THE PUPPY PROPOSAL

BY
KATIE MEYER

MILLS & BOON

Published in Great Britain 2015
by Mills & Boon, an imprint of Harlequin (UK) Limited,
Eton House, 18-24 Paradise Road, Richmond, Surrey, TW9 1SR

© 2015 Katie Meyer

ISBN: 978-0-263-25178-4

23-1015

Harlequin (UK) Limited's policy is to use papers that are natural, renewable and recyclable products and made from wood grown in sustainable forests. The logging and manufacturing processes conform to the legal environmental regulations of the country of origin.

Printed and bound in Spain
by CPI, Barcelona

"See this? His paws are raw.

"He's worn the pads right off. The hot, rough asphalt acts like sandpaper on them. Poor thing. . .that has to really hurt." Big blue eyes the color of a cloudless sky looked away from the dog and up at him. Eyes filled with sympathy and determination. "I'm going to call Dr Marshall. Murphy will need some pain medication, and maybe some antibiotics."

As he listened to her make arrangements, he let himself look his fill. The concern on her face did nothing to detract from her beauty. Pale blue eyes were a stark contrast to the mass of ebony curls attempting to escape the clip she'd secured it with. Her skin was fair, her cheekbones prominent, and then there was that mouth, those perfectly pink lips that she pursed when she was concentrating. A man would have to be blind not to want to kiss those lips.

That doctor had better show up soon; if he was alone with the sexy vet tech much longer, he might end up panting as badly as the dog in front of him.

* * *

Paradise Animal Clinic:
Let the love—and fur-ever families—fly!

Katie Meyer is a Florida native with a firm belief in happy endings. A former veterinary technician and dog trainer, she now spends her days homeschooling her children, writing and snuggling with her pets. Her guilty pleasures include good chocolate, *Downton Abbey* and cheap champagne. Preferably all at once. She looks to her parents' whirlwind romance and her own happy marriage for her romantic inspiration.

Dedicated to:

My parents for giving me a love of books, and my husband for telling me to write my own already.

All the friends that supported me, especially Jilda, Rebecca, Elizabeth, the ladies of The Well Trained Mind and the incredible women of Hearts on Paper.

All the wonderful veterinary professionals I've worked with, especially Mary C. Fondren, DVM, who supported me in countless ways over the years.

And of course, my agent Jill and the wonderful editorial team at Harlequin Special Edition, who took a chance on me.

Chapter One

He'd almost missed it. Had the setting sun been just a bit lower, the light a bit dimmer, he would have missed it, *it* being the most pathetic-looking animal he had ever seen. The dog—if that was the right word for the wet, filth-encrusted beast limping along the side of the road—was obviously in trouble. There wasn't much traffic right now on this stretch of highway, but the Paradise Isle Bridge was just ahead, or so said the tinny voice of his rental car's GPS. Crossing a highway bridge on foot, or paw for that matter, seemed a dangerous proposition. Besides, it was limping.

But limping or not, it wasn't his dog. Wasn't his problem. He was in a suit. In a rental car. On vacation—well, sort of a vacation. A working vacation. So this grimy creature was definitely not his problem.

Surely it knew the way home or would be picked up

by someone that actually lived around here. Not that he was exactly sure where here was, GPS or no. He hadn't passed a single town in over an hour, and the only brief glimpse of humanity had been a roadside stand selling gator jerky and boiled peanuts twenty miles back.

Nic Caruso tightened his grip on the steering wheel as he approached and then passed, telling himself the dog would be fine. But his gaze kept returning to the rearview mirror, where he watched the muddy stray as it slowly hobbled east. Then saw it flinch as a wave of dirty water thrown by a speeding car drenched it yet again.

"Damn it!"

Nic swung the small SUV to the shoulder, slammed to a stop and quickly located the emergency flashers on the unfamiliar dash. It might not be his problem or his responsibility, but he couldn't bring himself to just leave the dog there. Resigned, he undid his already loosened tie, carefully laying it on the suit jacket occupying the passenger's seat.

"Here, boy! Come here now." He used his most authoritative voice, the one that he relied on in boardrooms across the globe.

Nothing.

The darned dog just kept going. So much for doing this the easy way. Nic opened the passenger's door again and retrieved his tie. A quick slipknot and he had an impromptu leash. Great. Somehow, he didn't think Hermès would approve.

"Easy, boy. That's it. Eaaasy…" Nic inched his way across the muddy roadside toward the now cowering dog, careful not to spook him any closer to the highway.

A furry ear cocked in interest. The softer approach seemed to be working.

"Good boy. Come on, that's a good boy. How about I give you a ride wherever you're going, okay?"

A small tail wag was quickly followed by a cautious step forward. Hoping to appear less threatening, Nic crouched down, putting himself at eye level with the cautious canine. Brown eyes watched him warily, but the dog did keep moving in the right direction.

Only a foot away, cars sped by, but Nic kept his focus on the muddy beast in front of him, willing him to co-operate. Only a little bit farther and...

"Gotcha!"

Nic slid the improvised leash over the dog and held tight, just in case he bolted, but the bedraggled beast seemed to have lost his earlier apprehension. A happy, wriggling bundle, he licked and yipped in gratitude. The frenetic thank-you dance gave Nic an up-close study of what appeared to be a border collie—admittedly just a best guess with all the grime matting down his fur. He was a good size, maybe fifty pounds, but from the look of the large paws, he wasn't done growing yet.

"So what do we do now? Any ideas?"

An enthusiastic face-licking was hardly an appro-priate answer.

Nic stood and stretched while he thought of what to do. A week in the heart of Orlando on business, night-mare traffic on I-4, miles of desolate highway and now a muddy dog. When exactly had he completely lost con-trol of his life? The only thing he could think to do was to keep heading for the island, and hope there was a shelter or veterinary hospital still open. Resolved, he started walking the dog along the shoulder of the road, only to be stopped by a soft whimper. Crap. Crouching again, he gathered the grubby canine to his chest and lifted him up. Carrying him to the car, Nic tried to ignore the ooze seeping through his shirt.

"Up you go." Nic held the door open with one hand, and the makeshift leash with the other. No more encouragement was needed; the dog bounded into the rear seat easily. Hopefully, that meant he wasn't badly injured.

Rounding the car, Nic brushed the worst of the dirt and fur off his clothes before sitting behind the wheel. He checked his mirrors and pulled carefully back onto the highway, then rolled down his windows as soon as he was up to speed, hoping to keep the wet-dog smell from permeating the upholstery. He doubted rental insurance covered that particular contingency.

That was a mistake.

Tempted by the open window, the dog nimbly hopped into the front seat and shoved his muzzle into the rushing air. Nic cast a grin at the happy animal's expression—then cursed when he saw the now ruined suit jacket under his muddy paws.

Nic mumbled uncharitable remarks about the pup's parentage until the top of the Paradise Isle Bridge, where he was seduced into silence. From the apex of its span, he could see fishing boats bobbing among the diamond topped crests of the Intracoastal, then the lush green of the island, and beyond that the Atlantic Ocean, where pink-and-purple clouds flamed on the horizon, caught in the last rays of the setting sun. In his rearview mirror the atmospheric show continued, a kaleidoscope of colors, constantly shifting as the orange orb of the sun slipped further toward the horizon. The sight of all that sea and sky managed to melt the last of his workday tension, leaving him feeling, for the first time in a long time, almost free. Or he would be, once he figured out what to do with the dog.

* * *

"Yes, Mrs. Ellington, I can see how that would be upsetting." Veterinary technician Jillian Everett rubbed her temples with one hand while cradling the oversize phone receiver in the other. "But remember, Tinker Bell is only nine weeks old. It's perfectly normal for her to not be housebroken yet… Oh. Well, no, I'm afraid I don't know of any products that will get that kind of stain out of a leather handbag."

A loud snort of laughter betrayed Dr. Cassie Marshall's presence behind her.

"Yes, I agree, replacing it probably is the best idea. But, I really think you should consider waiting until Tinker Bell is older before carrying her in your purse for so long. When she's a bit bigger, she'll be better able to control where she, uh, leaves her presents. In the meantime, just stick to the feeding and training guidelines we sent home and I think she'll be fine. If you have any other questions, I'm sure Dr. Marshall would be happy to answer them at your appointment next week." Jillian mouthed a "gotcha" at Cassie, who was holding up her hands in a "not me" gesture.

"Okay, Mrs. Ellington, we'll see you next week. Have a good night and kiss little Tinker Bell for us. Bye." Jillian hung up and glared at Cassie. "You set me up! You knew what that call was about, didn't you? Why is she calling the veterinary hospital for a poopy purse, anyway? Don't those fancy dog purse things have liners for this sort of situation? Or an emergency number to call?" Shaking her head at the absurdity of the situation, she made a notation in the file and stood to put it in the appropriate place.

"I didn't set you up…exactly. After all, helping with the call tonight was your idea. But yes, Mollie may have hinted at the situation before she left, and I may have made sure that particular chart ended up with the ones you so generously took off my hands." She smiled. "Perk of being the boss, sorry."

Jillian didn't think Cassie's wide grin looked the least bit contrite. But she *was* a great boss, and Jillian *had* volunteered. Cassie had a young daughter to get home to, so when Jillian saw the big stack of files requiring follow-up phone calls, she had offered to take the majority of them. She planned to give Mollie, the receptionist at Paradise Animal Clinic, a piece of her mind tomorrow for that final absurd call, but really, it wasn't as if she had anywhere else to be. No one was waiting at home for her tonight. Or any night. Most of the time, the animal clinic was more of a home to her than her tiny apartment was.

She didn't have any family. Both of her parents had been killed in a car accident, and she'd been too young to really remember them. The last in a long line of her foster families had lived on Paradise Isle, and she had found a sense of belonging here that had kept her on the island long after she'd aged out of the system. She had never been adopted, but the people of Paradise Isle had become a kind of surrogate family. Most of the time, that was enough. But on nights like tonight, when she had nothing better to do than stay late and file charts, she couldn't help but daydream about someday having a real family to go home to.

"I'll lock up on my way out. See you in the morning," Cassie called from halfway out the door, juggling her keys, briefcase and a stack of veterinary trade magazines. She might be leaving the office, but Jillian knew she'd spend a few more hours working after her daughter, Emma, was asleep. Cassie was a single mom, and had taken over the clinic from her father, after he was permanently injured in a car accident a few years ago. Now her parents watched Emma during the day, doting on their only granddaughter, freeing Cassie to focus on the veterinary hospital. It was an arrangement born of necessity, but it worked because of their strong love for each other, something Jillian couldn't help but envy.

As she filed, the only sounds were the bubbling of the fish tank and the hiss of an overworked air conditioner fighting the Florida heat. A full day of barking dogs, hissing cats and chatty clients had her appreciating the temporary quiet, only for it to be broken minutes later by a banging at the front door. For a second she considered staying out of sight, behind the tall wall of files. People often stopped by after hours to try to pick up last-minute items, and she really didn't want to deal with that tonight. But, as always, her sense of duty won out.

Pulling her unruly black curls into a mostly serviceable ponytail, she forced a smile on her face, ready to serve whatever tardy client was making such a ruckus. Approaching the heavily tinted glass front door, she could make out, dimly, a very large man holding what appeared to be a squirming dog. Medical instincts kicked in at the sight of the would-be patient, spurring her to run the last few steps to unlock and open the door. Standing behind it was a seemingly solid wall of muscular man. Ignoring him, and her suddenly rapid heartbeat, she focused instead on the very familiar-looking dog.

"Oh, no, is that Murphy? What happened? Is he hurt?" Her voice came out more forcefully than she'd intended, but the shock of seeing her favorite patient being carried in by a stranger had her protective instincts kicking into high gear. She tried to assess the dog, but the man holding him was so tall it was hard to get a good look.

"I have no idea who or what a Murphy is, but I found this mongrel on the side of the highway as I was driving into town." He shifted the dog, holding him away from what had once been a white dress shirt. "I don't think he's hurt too badly, but he definitely needs a bath."

Jillian relaxed a bit, her mouth twitching up despite her worry. The guy, whoever he was, made quite a picture holding the pathetic dog in his arms. He was tall, over six feet, dark hair and eyes, with broad shoulders that filled out his business clothes well. The bristly stubble starting to show only added to his masculine aura. That he was carrying the nearly fully grown dog without visible signs of strain impressed her. That he had stopped to rescue the dog at all impressed her even more.

"So…are you going to help him?" the man asked, eyebrows raised. He probably wondered why she was just standing there, staring up at him like a fool.

"Oh, um, yes. Let me take a look, see if I need to call the vet back in. Just bring him in here." Jillian snapped back into work mode, chiding herself for ogling when there was an animal that needed help. Motioning him into an exam room, she told herself she was a professional. And professionals were not supposed to check out the client's rear end, no matter how nice it was.

Chapter Two

Nic carried the dog into the small, spotlessly clean room, gently lowering him onto the slick exam table. Immediately the troublemaker tried to jump off into Jillian's arms. "Oh, no you don't. Stay," he said, grabbing the squirming dog before he could take flight.

"Good reflexes," she commented, smiling that pretty smile again.

"Years of wrestling with my younger brother," he answered. "You said you might need to call the vet. I thought you were the vet." Confused, he pointedly looked at her scrubs. Scrubs that did nothing to hide her feminine curves.

"Me? No, I'm the veterinary technician, Jillian Everett," she corrected. "Cassie—I mean, Dr. Marshall—already left. But let me take a look, and then I'll give her a call if there's anything wrong." She opened a drawer below the gleaming examining table and removed a small scanning device. "But first, let's see who this furry guy is. I'm pretty positive it's Murphy, Mrs. Rosenberg's border collie, but a microchip would tell us for sure. Hopefully we'll luck out, and the scanner will be able to find one."

Upon hearing his name, the dog whimpered, wriggling in delight.

"I think you just got your answer as to who he is. And speaking of names, I'm Nic."

"You're probably right, Nic, but let's do this by the book, just in case." She held down a button and ran the scanner up and down the dog's neck, stroking his black-and-white fur with her other hand. Her affection for the dog was obvious. When the machine beeped, she wrote down a number that had popped up on the screen. "I've got Murphy's chip number recorded in his file. Let me get it and I'll be right back."

Left alone with the dog, Nic found himself hoping the veterinary tech would come back soon. He liked her smile, and the way her dark curls kept falling across her face. Liked the gentle way she stroked the dog without seeming to notice she was doing it. He wondered if those hands felt as soft as they looked. But mostly, he liked that she was focused on the dog, not him. Fawning women had become a huge turnoff.

"It's definitely Murphy," she said, striding back into the room. Murphy squirmed in glee, as if happy to be recognized. "All right, boy, I know you're happy to see me. I'm happy to see you, too. But I've got to make sure you're not hurt, okay, handsome?" She ran her hands along the dog's back and along his sides, feeling through the thick coat. "Murphy's a favorite of mine, smarter than most dogs, but as likely to get into trouble as his name implies."

"His name?" Nic looked down at the dog in his arms, confused.

"Murphy. As in Murphy's Law?" She picked up the front leg and continued to check him over for any obvious open wounds or signs of pain.

"Ah, I take it this isn't his first misadventure, then?" Nic could relate to that. He'd had his own stretch of mishaps growing up.

"Oh, no, Murphy makes trouble his hobby. It's really not his fault—he's just a smart, active dog without enough to keep him busy. Border collies are herding dogs—they need a job to do, some way to channel their energy. Mrs. Rosenberg is very nice, but she's in her seventies and just not up to giving him the kind of exercise and training he needs. So our boy here finds his own exercise. He's broken out of her apartment a few times before, but I've never known him to make it all the way over the bridge. That's quite a hike, even for an athletic dog like Murphy."

Annoyed by the owner's lack of forethought, he asked, "If she can't keep up with him, why did she get him in the first place?" His whole life was nothing but responsibilities; the idea of someone being so irresponsible, even with a pet, rankled him.

"She didn't, not exactly. Her son, who wouldn't know a collie from a cockatiel, gave him to her for a present. Said a dog would keep her company. As if she needed company—she's a member of every committee and social group in town. She tried to talk me into taking him, but my apartment building doesn't allow dogs." She paused, bent down to look at something more closely and then frowned. "Nic, can you hold him on his side for

me, lying down? I want to get a better look at his paws.
I think I know why he was limping."

Nic complied, concerned that she might have found
something serious. Had he missed something? He hadn't
stopped to check the dog over before getting back on the
road. His only thought had been to find somewhere that
would take the dog off his hands. When he saw the sign
for the Paradise Animal Clinic just past the bridge, it
had seemed a good bet. Second-guessing his handling
of the situation, he gently but firmly turned the dog on
his side, careful not to hurt or scare him. Then, while he
held the dog in place, Jillian carefully checked each paw.

"See this? His paws are raw. He's worn the pads right
off. The hot, rough asphalt acts like sandpaper on them.
Poor thing…that has to really hurt." Big blue eyes the
color of a cloudless sky looked away from the dog and
up at him. Eyes filled with sympathy and determination. "I'm going to call Dr. Marshall. Murphy will need
some pain medication, and maybe some antibiotics." She
picked up a phone hung on the back wall of the small
room and placed the call. "Hi, Cassie…yes, I'm still
here. We've got a little problem. Murphy Rosenberg is
here. Someone found him on the side of the road again.
He seems to be in good shape for the most part, but he's
really done a number on his paws this time. I think you'd
better come take a look."

As he listened to her make arrangements, he let himself look his fill. The concern on her face did nothing to
detract from her beauty. Pale blue eyes were a stark contrast to the mass of ebony curls attempting to escape the
clip she'd secured it with. Her skin was fair, her cheekbones prominent, and then there was that mouth, those
perfectly pink lips that she pursed when she was con-

centrating. A man would have to be blind not to want to kiss those lips.

That doctor had better show up soon; if he was alone with the sexy vet tech much longer, he might end up panting as badly as the dog in front of him.

Jillian hung up the phone, relieved that help was on the way. And not just for Murphy's sake. Being alone with his rescuer was making her a bit nervous. Not that she was afraid of him; she couldn't be afraid of someone willing to stop and help an injured animal the way he had. He just made her…uneasy. Especially when he looked at her with those intense brown eyes, as if he were examining her, looking inside her. Raising her chin, hoping she projected more confidence than she felt, she asked, "Can you carry him into the treatment room for me? We can clean him up a bit while we're waiting."

He easily lifted the dog, once again making the movement look effortless. "Just show me where."

Jillian held the rear exam room door open, allowing him to pass through into the heart of the veterinary hospital. She wondered how it appeared to him. To her the stretches of gleaming chrome and spotless countertops, the bank of cages filling the back wall, the tangy scent of disinfectant were all more familiar than her own apartment. However, she knew the microscopes, centrifuges and bright lights could be intimidating to the uninitiated. Some people actually got a bit queasy. But Nic, who was waiting patiently for her to indicate where to place the dog, seemed unaffected by the medical surroundings.

Pleased by his composure, she pointed to the long, shallow treatment basin covered by a steel grate. The six-foot-long sink was table height, and would allow her to bathe the dog carefully while checking for any other wounds she might have missed. He placed the dog on the grating, and Murphy, no stranger to a bath, behaved himself as she uncurled the spray handle from the end of the table, then rinsed and lathered.

Nic made an excellent assistant; he had rolled up his sleeves, exposing tanned, well-defined forearms that easily maneuvered the soapy canine according to her direction. Thankfully, she could lather and rinse the pleasant-smelling suds on autopilot, because those muscled arms were proving quite the distraction. Worried he might have noticed her staring, she bent down to retrieve a clean towel from the stacks kept below the sink. She tried to focus on toweling the dog off, rather than on the larger-than-life man across the table. But he wasn't making it easy.

"I hope you don't mind," Nic said, unbuttoning his shirt. "This thing smells like, well, wet dog." He shrugged out of the wet, muddy fabric with a grimace, leaving him standing in an almost as damp, but considerably cleaner, sleeveless undershirt and dress slacks.

Jillian nodded, eyes drawn to his broad, bare shoulders, then down to the impressive biceps that had restrained Murphy so easily. The revealed bronze skin spoke more of Mediterranean ancestry than hours in the sun. The tight undershirt did little to hide the chiseled chest underneath or the flat abdominals below. She might have continued to stare, basking in all that male beauty, if the sound of the front door hadn't snapped her back to reality.

"Jillian! Jillian! Where's the doggy? Is he hurt? Can I kiss his boo-boo? Who's that?" Emma Marshall, four years old and the spitting image of her mother, barreled into the room. Her strawberry-blond ponytail swished as she looked from Emma to Nic, blue eyes blinking rapidly.

"Emma, I told you that someone found a doggy and brought him here so I could help him." Cassie appeared in the doorway behind her rambunctious tyke. "Hi, I'm Dr. Marshall. Thank you for helping our Murphy here. I'm afraid he's a repeat offender, but we all love him, anyway."

"I'm Nic." Brushing away the compliment, he offered a tired smile and said, "He seems like a nice dog, now that he's cleaned up."

"Murphy was a mess when Nic brought him in, covered in mud and God knows what else. He helped me bathe him, but his shirt was a casualty," Jillian explained.

"My shirt, my tie and my suit jacket. But, hey, who's counting?" Nic shrugged his shoulders, and then returned his attention to the women in the room. "Can you do something for his paws? They look pretty awful."

Cassie moved to the table and gently examined each of the dog's feet. "They do look pretty bad, but they'll heal quickly. I'll give him an antibiotic injection to prevent infection, and he can have some anti-inflammatories to help with the pain. Beef-flavored tablets, he'll love them." Cassie drew up a syringe of milky-looking fluid. "You aren't squeamish around needles, are you?" she asked, cocking an eyebrow.

"Not at all." Nic eyed the syringe. "But shouldn't you be calling his owner? She's got to be missing him by now, right?" Nic looked first at Cassie, then at Jillian. "Shouldn't she have to approve treatment or something?"

"Normally, yes," Jillian answered. "But we have a standing permission for treatment in Murphy's chart.

Remember, this isn't his first time getting away. Besides, Mrs. Rosenberg won't be home tonight. She's over near Orlando on an overnight trip with her seniors group. She mentioned it to me when she stopped in to buy dog food yesterday. Murphy will have to stay here tonight, I guess." She grimaced. "I hate leaving him. If he scratches at the cage door, he's going to make his paws worse, and after his big outing, I'd rather he have someone keeping an eye on him. But my apartment manager won't allow me to take him home, and Cassie—I mean, Dr. Marshall—is currently fostering a dog at her house that doesn't get along with others. He'd beat poor Murphy up. So he'll have to stay here until Mrs. Rosenberg gets home."

Nic's eyebrows narrowed. "You're going to just put him in a cage?"

Cassie responded matter-of-factly, "It's not ideal, but he'll be safe—a lot safer than he was a few hours ago, thanks to you. There really isn't any other option."

"Yes, there is." Nic was firm, arms crossed. "He can stay with me. The Sandpiper Inn is pet-friendly, and I can bring him back here in the morning or to wherever you say to take him. I'll keep an eye on him, give him his medication and make sure he's okay overnight." His eyes dared anyone to disagree. "I didn't go through all the trouble of rescuing him to abandon him in the end."

"I don't think that will work…we don't even know you. Mrs. Rosenberg doesn't know you…" Jillian floundered. In her wildest dreams, she would never have expected this man to offer to play nursemaid to a gimpy dog. Knights in shining armor might be the norm in storybooks, but that kind of thing didn't happen in real life. Saviors, she knew from personal experience, were few and far between.

Cassie stepped in. "Why don't I call Mrs. Rosenberg and see what she has to say? We'll let her decide." Turning to Nic, she continued, "I'll need your contact information, and you'll have to fill out some paperwork, if she agrees. Does that sound all right?"

Nic nodded in agreement, still standing stiffly, as if ready to defend his newly found canine friend physically, if need be.

While he and Cassie worked out the arrangements, Jillian clung to the soft dog. She had lost control of this situation somehow, not something she generally let happen. Watching the gorgeous man in front her, she wondered what kind of man did this, dropped everything and did whatever it took to save the day. As if sensing her bewilderment, Murphy squirmed in her arms.

Comforting herself as much as the dog, she buried her face in his fur. The dog turned his head, straining to keep Nic in view, something he had done since the minute they'd arrived. "I know how you feel," she whispered in the smitten animal's ear. "I know how you feel."

Nic pulled into the parking lot of the Sandpiper Inn and turned the key, content to sit for a few minutes before he had to wrangle the dog and luggage. He still couldn't quite believe he had acquired a pet, yet another responsibility, even if it was just for the night. But he couldn't have left him in a cage, scared and hurt, any more than he could have left him on the side of the road.

At some point, taking on responsibility, taking care of others, had become second nature. He had always been the one to get his kid brother out of trouble, even when it meant getting into trouble himself. Later, he had tutored his sister, taking it upon himself to make sure she passed the dreaded algebra class. Then, after graduation, it had been impossible to say no to a job working for his father, eventually ending up where he was now, Nic Caruso, Vice President of Property Acquisitions at Caruso Hotels. The internationally known chain had been his father's dream, not his, and he found no joy in traveling from city to city, scouting out properties and securing new locations for the ever-growing company. He often wondered what it would be like to settle down in one place, to meet someone that appreciated him for who he was, rather than what he could provide.

A soft woof from the passenger's seat brought him out of his daydreams and into the present. "Don't worry, I'm coming. I didn't forget about you." Grabbing his overnight bag, Nic set out with Murphy across the covered breezeway connecting the parking area to the main house. In front of him the inn rose out of the darkness, spotlighted by the moon against the dunes behind it. It was hard to see details this late, but he knew from his research that it was two stories, built in the Florida Vernacular style. The buff-colored wooden siding would blend with the dunes in the daylight, and there were covered, whitewashed porches on every level, designed to offer a cool spot to enjoy the ocean view. Right now, though, all he could make out were the wide front steps and a welcoming glow from several of the shutter-framed windows.

Before continuing toward the inn, he took the sandy path that ran parallel to the dunes. Whether the inn was pet-friendly or not, he'd better give Murphy a chance to relieve himself before going in and getting settled.

As they walked, Nic was impressed by the sheer size of the grounds, which were crisscrossed by walking paths and planted with a variety of tropical and coastal scrub plants. He stopped to lean against one of the many smooth-trunked palms, breathing in the humid air, richly scented by the jasmine that grew heavy around him. The scent reminded him of the vet tech he'd just met, Jillian. Even over the disinfectant and wet-dog smells, he had picked up on her flowery sweetness, some perfume or shampoo or something.

Straightening, he tugged on the leash and walked back to the hotel entrance. He wasn't here to daydream about pretty brunettes or to soak up the night air. He had a location to scout. Caruso Hotels was very interested in this bit of land, and he was tasked with determining if they should make an offer to the current owners.

There was plenty of room here for a modern beach-front resort once the original inn was torn down. Most of the property was underutilized, a diamond in the rough. A high-rise hotel could change the entire community—bring in tourist dollars, chain retailers and more. A Caruso Hotel would move the town into the modern age, make it a hot spot on the Florida coast.

At the top of the stairs, the large carved door of the Sandpiper Inn opened smoothly, bringing him into the lobby, an eclectically decorated but surprisingly elegant room. Native pine floors gleamed in the light of an old-fashioned chandelier. An antique table to his right served as the check-in desk, and across the room over-stuffed furniture offered a cozy place to read or chat. Bay windows with a view of the night sea were directly opposite him; a native coquina fireplace accented the wall to the left.

Bookcases held everything from leather-bound tomes to contemporary bestsellers, with conch shells and chunks of coral for bookends. The antique and modern mix was nothing like the seamless, well- planned lobby of a Caruso Hotel, but welcoming in a way no modern resort could match. For once, he felt like he was stepping into something real, a true home away from home, instead of yet another commercial space.

"Are you checking in?" The question startled him for a moment, returning him to the present business. A young girl—she couldn't be more than eighteen—had come in from a doorway behind the check-in desk.

"Yes, Dominic Caruso. I have a reservation."

She tapped keys on a slim laptop computer, concentrating on the screen in front of her. "I don't see mention of a pet in the reservation notes. Will the dog be staying with you?"

"Yes, but only for one night. Is that a problem? Your website did say you were pet-friendly."

"Oh, no problem. I'll just send up a dog bed and some bowls for him. We have a small selection of pet food, as well, if you'd like." She smiled at Murphy, ignoring Nic in favor of his canine companion, and was rewarded by a mannerly wag of the tail.

"No, thank you, that won't be necessary." Jillian had fed Murphy some kibble before they left the clinic, and had packed him some more for the morning.

"Okay, sign here, then. You're in room 206, just up the stairs and to the left. Breakfast is served on the patio from seven to nine, and coffee and tea are always available in the sitting room. If you need anything, just let me know."

"Thank you very much. I'm sure we'll be fine." He pocketed the key, a real key, not a plastic key card, and headed up the staircase he had passed when he came in. The finely carved banister was smooth beneath his hand, worn to a soft glow by generations of guests and hours of polishing. Upstairs, the hall was quiet and softly lit; most of the other guests were probably sleeping, or perhaps out for a late stroll on the beach.

Grateful for the quiet, he let himself into the compact but tasteful room she had assigned him. Too tired to note much of his surroundings, he stripped off his filthy clothes on the way to the shower, where he stood under the hot, stinging spray to rinse off the mud, sweat and stress of the day. Resting his head on the cool tile, he let the water massage his back and tried to think of nothing, to just be. Instead, his thoughts kept circling back to Jillian, to her pale blue eyes, dark ringlets and those perfect, kissable lips. In a different place, a different time, he would love to explore those lips, and maybe more. But no, he had to work. Hell, he always had to work. At least he was good at his job. Dating, on the other hand, was a series of disasters. It seemed he had a target on his back visible to every gold digger for a hundred miles. His brother adored the attention the family name brought, but as far as Nic was concerned, being single was better than being used.

Annoyed, he turned the faucet to cold, hoping to clear his head. When even that didn't work, he toweled off, then collapsed on the big antique bed. Maybe it was the soft snores of the dog at the foot of the bed. Maybe it was the lull of the waves outside his window. Or maybe he was just that tired. Whatever the reason, for once he didn't have to fight his usual travel-induced insomnia. Tonight, sleep came quickly, the kind of dreamless deep sleep that only came to him when he was home.

Chapter Three

Jillian's morning was a blur of fur and files. There had been countless puppy kisses, but she had also been bitten, scratched and peed on. And that was only the first appointment—new puppy exams for a pair of Labradoodles. Since then, she had struggled to balance her time between assisting in the exam rooms, completing vital laboratory work and counseling owners on proper pet care. Officially, the clinic closed at noon on Saturdays, but it was already almost one, and she still had charts to write up before she left.

Grabbing a diet soda from the break room, she sat at the back desk, away from the barking and hissing, with her stack of charts. But no matter how hard she tried to concentrate, her mind kept returning to Murphy and, if she was honest, to the man who had found him. Lots of men came through the clinic, but not many looked like some kind of Roman god.

And as if being gorgeous wasn't enough, his compassion toward Murphy had bumped him up even higher on the sexy stranger scale of attraction. She had forgotten to ask him what had brought him to town. She knew he wasn't a regular; Paradise was so small, she'd have heard about him if he had been here long. No, more than likely he was one of the few vacationers that occasionally found their way to Paradise.

The island definitely didn't qualify as a tourist mecca; there were no giant, high-end resorts, nightclubs or theme parks to draw people in. But the beaches were pristine, and half the island was a dedicated wildlife refuge, so they did get the occasional nature lover. Somehow, though, Jillian couldn't quite picture the well-dressed man she'd met last night as a bird watcher.

She sighed. Not thinking about him wasn't working; maybe she should be proactive instead. Mrs. Rosenberg should be home by now. If she was fast, she could pick Murphy up at the inn, get him back to his owner and still have time to grab a quick bite before the meeting of the Island Preservation Society this afternoon. Once the Murphy situation was handled, she could move on and stop thinking about the mysterious Nic.

Decided, she grabbed the phone and dialed Mrs. Rosenberg's cell phone number. "Hi, Mrs. Rosenberg. It's Jillian. I'm just finishing up here at work, and wanted to let you know I'll be by with Murphy shortly."

"Oh, dear, I was just about to call you. There's been a slight change in plans. We girls decided to stop over at the outlet malls on the way back, and then, before we knew it, we were at that all-you-can-eat steakhouse. We've given our credit cards a workout, I'm afraid. But as soon as we finish lunch we'll be on our way. I should be in town before three, and you and Murphy and I can have a nice visit then. I'll make us some sangria with a wonderful red I picked up on the winery tour."

"I'm afraid I'll have to take a rain check on that sangria, Mrs. Rosenberg. The Island Preservation Society meeting is this afternoon. I need to head there right after work." Jillian twisted the phone cord, thrown off by the change of plans. "I can bring Murphy by after the meeting, as long as that isn't too late for you. I think we should wrap up by dinnertime."

"That's fine, dear. I can't wait to see my naughty boy. I'm so glad he's okay. I do hate how he keeps getting into scrapes. Won't you reconsider keeping him? I'd feel so much better if he was with someone young and energetic like you."

The elderly woman's request tugged at Jillian's heartstrings. She loved that dog, but there was no way she could keep him. "I'm sorry, Mrs. Rosenberg, you know I'd love to, but my landlord won't allow it. Maybe when my lease is up…" But that was just wishful thinking. Paradise Isle didn't have many apartment buildings, and none allowed dogs Murphy's size. Renting or buying a house was out of the question on her current salary.

Somehow, she, the girl who had grown up wanting nothing more than a houseful of kids and pets, had ended up alone in a small apartment, without so much as a goldfish. That was why she had joined the Island Preservation Society. If she couldn't have the Norman Rockwell life she'd always wanted, she'd have to settle for protecting her picture-perfect community instead. Paradise Isle was her home, and people like Mrs. Rosenberg were her family. "I'll call you when I'm on my way. Have a safe drive back."

"I'll try, but Avril Clookie is driving this time, and you know what a flighty young thing she is."

Mrs. Clookie was at least sixty years old, and about as flighty as a St. Bernard, but Jillian let it go. After saying her goodbyes, she found the consent form Nic had signed last night. His full name was Dominic Caruso, which sounded familiar somehow, and he'd left both his room number at the inn and his cell phone number in the contact section. When he didn't answer at the room number, she dialed the cell.

"Hello?" He sounded out of breath, and she could hear wind blowing in the background.

"Hi, Nic, it's Jillian."

"Ready to pick up your patient?"

"Actually, there's been a change in plans. It seems Mrs. Rosenberg won't be back for a few more hours. I have a meeting after work, so it would probably be best if you brought him to the clinic. I can leave him here while I'm at the meeting, then take him home after that. I'm sorry to change things up on you." She hoped he wasn't too annoyed by the change of plans; his corporate look had screamed "type-A personality" last night.

"No problem. I just finished a run on the beach, figured I'd get some exercise while I was waiting to hear from you. If you want, I can—"

"Wait, you took Murphy running on the beach? His paws haven't healed! He shouldn't—"

"Whoa, slow down! Murphy's upstairs sleeping, more than likely in my bed. I've only taken him out long enough to do his business, and I even rinsed his paws off afterward." Nic's voice was harsh, and Jillian felt herself flush. She shouldn't have assumed. "I'm not an idiot—I do know how to take care of a dog."

"You're right, and I'm sorry. I'm just annoyed that I couldn't take care of Murphy myself. I'm grateful you offered to take him in—really, I am. I'm afraid I let myself get flustered by the whole switch in plans. I hope all this hasn't been too much of an inconvenience."

"It's fine. But listen, I still don't like leaving him in a cage. Why don't you just give me his owner's address, and I'll take him there myself? That way she gets her dog back and you can go to your...what was it?"

"A meeting over at the library. But really, I could figure something out. You've done more than enough already."

"I wouldn't offer if I didn't mean it. I'd like to see him safely home, if that's okay. We've bonded."

"Bonded, huh?" She felt herself smiling; he seemed to have that effect on her.

"Sleeping together does that," Nic deadpanned. "He's a cover hog—don't let him tell you otherwise."

The image of Nic in bed, dog or no dog, was one Jillian did not need in her head. "Fine, I'll give Mrs. Rosenberg your number. If it's okay with her, she'll call you and give you her address, arrange a time." Jillian paused, "I really do appreciate everything you've done for Murphy."

"Well, if that's the case, there is a way you could pay me back."

"How?" Maybe he wasn't so altruistic, after all. If he was looking for a reward, he was out of luck; neither she nor Mrs. Rosenberg had the extra cash.

"Have dinner with me."

"Dinner?" Her jaw dropped.

"Yeah, you know, the meal after lunch? I'm assuming your meeting will be over by then. I thought you could take me somewhere interesting, somewhere the locals go."

"Well…the locals mainly eat at Pete's. It's not fancy, but they have great burgers, and the seafood is fresh." Jillian tried to picture Nic in his business suit in the more-than-rustic atmosphere of Pete's. "Or we could go to the mainland. There are plenty of restaurants over there, nicer places—"

"Pete's sounds great, exactly what I'm in the mood for. Where can I pick you up?"

"I'll pick you up, at the Sandpiper," she countered. Even small-town girls knew not to get in a stranger's car. "Is six thirty okay? The deck fills up fast on a Saturday night."

"Perfect, it's a date. I'll see you then." A telltale click signaled the end of the call.

She hung up the phone slowly. A date? Since when did she go on dates with random strangers, no matter how sexy they were?

At three o'clock that afternoon, Nic was parked outside a small pink stucco house with a very eager border collie. Murphy strained at the leash on the way up the front walk, apparently as eager to go home as he had been to escape. Nic rang the bell and tried to quiet the dog. Almost immediately, the door was opened by a diminutive woman in a teal tracksuit and rhinestone glasses. Her close-cropped hair was a shade of red that was not, and never had been, anyone's natural color. Nearly blinded by the combination, he was caught off guard when she dove in for a hug, her short stature leaving her head resting just above his navel.

"Thank you! Thank you! Thank you!" Each thank-you was punctuated by a surprisingly strong squeeze.

"You saved my precious baby. My sweet boy. Such a sweet, naughty, naughty boy!" With that, she crouched down to hug the canine in question. Murphy, for his part, took the praise as no more than his due.

Finished with her exuberant greeting, she straightened to her full height, which he guessed to be no more than four and a half feet, and tugged on his hand. "Come in, come in. I'm about to open some fabulous wine that I found on my trip. You must have a glass and tell me everything that happened."

Nic followed, intrigued by the tiny dynamo. He knew Florida was known for its active senior lifestyle, but he had a feeling Mrs. Rosenberg surpassed even that stereotype. Besides, he wanted to find out how Murphy was pulling his little escape act.

The house was immaculate, and filled with overstuffed furniture in shades of mauve and teal. Paintings of tropical flowers were on the walls, and a large brass manatee served as a centerpiece atop the glass coffee table. Through the doorway to the right he could see a small galley kitchen; shopping bags currently covered every inch of counter space.

His hostess dug through the bags, removing multiple bottles of wine before finding what she was looking for. Her wrinkled but capable hands deftly wielded the corkscrew, then poured them each a generous portion. He accepted the proffered glass and took a seat on the overlarge love seat, sinking into the soft surface. His hostess's much smaller body perched on the chair across from him as she raised her glass to toast. "To Murphy!"

"To Murphy." He sipped cautiously. It was surprisingly sweet, but certainly drinkable.

"Good, isn't it? Grown right here in Florida. It's made

with native grapes. Lots of antioxidants." She winked, then drank.

He nodded, not sure what to say to the winking, booze-pushing senior in front of him.

"So you found my boy. Jillian says he was all the way across the bridge this time! I am in your debt, son—if you hadn't stopped, there's no telling what could have happened to him. A car could have gotten him, or an alligator! We have those here, you know."

Nic did know, but hadn't thought about it at the time. Which was probably a good thing. Changing the subject, he asked, "Mrs. Rosenberg, do you know how Murphy escaped? Jillian said this wasn't his first attempt. I'd hate to see him get out again."

She shook her head, neon hair flying wildly. "It's a mystery to me. I left him locked in the house, with his food and water. The neighbor was going to let him out for me at bedtime, but she says he was already gone. If he'd been outside, I might think he dug out, since he's done that before, but from inside the house? That doesn't seem likely." She frowned in thought, her bedazzled spectacles sliding down her nose.

"Do you mind if I look around, see if I can find his escape route?"

"Look wherever you like, son. I'll just sit here and finish my wine." She took another healthy swig. "You let me know if you find anything."

Curiosity getting the better of him, Nic decided to start at the front of the house. Murphy, who'd been lying happily at his feet, jumped up, eager to follow wherever he led. The front door offered no clues, and the windows appeared secure. No loose locks or broken panes. The bedroom windows were the same. Murphy, thinking there was some game afoot, pranced and barked as he searched.

When they got to the kitchen, the dog ran ahead and jumped up onto the kitchen door. Wondering, Nic stopped, and watched. Sure enough, Murphy jumped again, this time his paws hitting the lever door handle. If the dead bolt hadn't been in place, the door would have popped right open. "Mrs. Rosenberg, was the kitchen door dead bolted when you were away?"

"The kitchen door? No, the key for that lock got lost a long time ago. But I did push the button in, on the doorknob. That locks it from the inside, and it opens with the same key as the front door." She paused, eyes wide, "You don't think someone broke in, do you?"

"No, not a break-in," he assured her. "Just a breakout. See these scratches on the door? I think Murphy was jumping at the door to follow you, and his paws landed on the handle. That lock opens automatically from the inside as soon as you turn the handle. He just let himself right out. Then I imagine the storm blew it shut again. If you're going to keep him in, you're going have replace that lever-style handle with a good old-fashioned doorknob."

"Oh, my goodness. What a smart boy! Opening doors!" Mrs. Rosenberg beamed at her black-and-white escape artist. "But I see what you mean. We can't have him gallivanting around town. I'll have to ask around about a handyman—I'm afraid tools and such just aren't my area of expertise."

"I could do it," Nic said before he could stop himself.

"Would you? Oh, that would be such a load off my mind. I worry so about poor Murphy. I know this isn't the best home for him, but I'd be sick if anything happened to him." Before Nic could think of a way to extricate himself, she pressed a wad of cash into his hands. "Palm Hardware is just around the corner. You must have passed it on the way here. Just pick out whatever you think is best."

Thirty minutes later, Nic was tightening the last screw with, of all things, a pink screwdriver. Murphy had been banished to the bedroom after getting in the way a few too many times, and Mrs. Rosenberg was thrilled. Straightening, he couldn't help but grin as he packed up the pastel tool kit. Project Dog-Proof was a success, and despite his initial reluctance to get involved, it felt good to know he'd been able to help. Getting his own hands dirty was a lot more satisfying than just signing a work order.

"I have to say, I'm so glad Jillian had that meeting today, and you came instead. Not that I don't love Jillian," she clarified hastily. "Murphy adores her and I do, too. But I wouldn't have felt right asking her to change a doorknob. I'm a bit too old-fashioned for that."

He grinned. Of all the ways he might describe Mrs. Rosenberg, "old-fashioned" wasn't one of them. "What sort of meeting she was going to?" He told himself he was only interested as part of his research on the island. He certainly wasn't prying into the pretty vet tech's life. Not very much, anyway.

"The Island Preservation Society. Jillian is one of the founding members," Mrs. Rosenberg said proudly. "I don't attend the meetings—meetings give me heartburn—but I donate when they have their annual rummage sale, and attend the dinner dance they do in the spring."

His shoulders tensed. "What exactly does this society do?"

"They mostly work to preserve the historic buildings, protect the coastal habitat, anything that has to do with maintaining the way of life Paradise is known for." Her eyes shined with pride. "Our little town isn't as fancy or popular as Daytona or Miami or those other beach places, and that's just fine with us. We like things the way they are, if you know what I mean."

Nic was afraid he did know. From what she was saying, he was going to have a fight on his hands, and Jillian was playing for the other side.

Jillian walked quickly across the hot asphalt parking lot, sticky with sweat and humidity. Ahead, the air-conditioned coolness of the Palmetto County Library beckoned like a mirage, a refuge from the last gasp of summer. Stepping inside, she took a deep breath, embracing the smell of old books that permeated the air. Fortified, she climbed the single staircase to the crowded conference room where Cassie and Mollie were waiting for her.

"We saved you a seat." Mollie waved, her pixie-like face lighting up at the sight of her friend. "I was afraid you wouldn't show, and you know I only come to these things because of you." Formal meetings of any sort were definitely not Mollie's thing. Grateful, Jillian hugged the petite woman in appreciation.

"I appreciate you making the sacrifice. These meetings really are important, especially now. Rumor is that the Sandpiper's new owner wants to sell."

"Sell the Sandpiper Inn? That place is an institution! I can remember Dad taking me there as a kid for the annual fish fry and the Christmas tree lighting ceremony. And just a few years ago, he and mom had their twenty-fifth anniversary party there." Cassie's eyebrows furrowed. "It's bad enough that they don't do the community events anymore, but sell it? To who?"

"I don't know." She shrugged. "They haven't even officially put it on the market yet. I think that happens Monday. I only know about it because another one of the Island Preservation Society members, Edward Post, told me about it when I saw him at the grocery store yesterday. He was always close with the Landry family, and had hoped when their daughter inherited the Sandpiper she would bring it back to its glory days. But she's got her own retail shop over in Orlando, and isn't interested in being an innkeeper. He thinks she'll take the first good offer she gets."

Jillian's heart hurt just thinking of the stately inn being taken over by outsiders, or worse, torn down. A beacon on the Paradise Isle shoreline, the Sandpiper had stood for more than a century. Its spacious grounds had always served as an unofficial community center, the gregarious owners often hosting holiday events, weddings, even a prom or two. She'd fallen in love with the grand building the first time she saw it and had always imagined she'd bring her own family to events there, one day. Now it might be destroyed before she ever had that chance. It just didn't seem fair, or right, to let it slip away without a fight.

As the meeting got under way, she found it hard to concentrate on the details of the historic post office renovation, or a proposal for a bike lane on Island Avenue. Normally she was the first volunteer for a Society project, but right now she was too on edge about the fate of the Sandpiper Inn.

And if she was honest with herself, the issue with the

Sandpiper wasn't the only thing making her palms sweat. A good number of the butterflies fluttering in her stomach were about her upcoming date. It wasn't as if she'd never been on a date before; at twenty-seven, she'd had her share of relationships. But always with local, familiar, safe men. Nothing serious. After a few dates, they'd ended up just friends, leaving her wondering if she was even capable of more intense feelings.

But Nic, with his towering good looks and confident manner, was another kind of man altogether. One that had her squirming in her seat, unsure if she was eager for the meeting to be over or afraid of what came after it.

Finally, the last item on the agenda was addressed. Edward Post stood at the front of the room, faced the folding chairs and cleared his throat. "I know that a few of you have heard rumors about the Sandpiper Inn. I'm afraid those rumors have been confirmed. Ms. Roberta Landry, the current owner, has decided to sell the inn and return to her job in Orlando." Shifting his weight nervously, he continued, "The board of the Island Preservation Society has spoken with Ms. Landry, and she has agreed to at least entertain the idea of the city purchasing the inn for community use."

"Can the city afford to buy it?" someone from the crowd asked.

Edward pushed his glasses up his nose, to see who had spoken. "No, not without help. We're preparing an application to the State Register of Historic Places. If we can get the Sandpiper listed, we may be able to get a grant toward its preservation, which would help offset the purchase price. Our chances are good, but the process can take several months. If there is another offer before that happens, Ms. Landry is within her rights to sell without waiting for the outcome of our application."

At that point the meeting broke down, voices rising as friends and families discussed the odds of success. Everyone already knew, without being told, that with land prices finally going up, a new owner was likely to raze the inn and parcel the land up.

Heartsick, Jillian avoided the speculating citizens and quietly made her goodbyes. Descending the stairs, she vowed to contact Edward and volunteer to write the grant application herself. Tonight she'd start researching the process, figure out their best way forward. She was going to do whatever she could to increase their chances of getting that grant. This was her home, and she wasn't giving up without a fight.

Chapter Four

Nic waited for Jillian on the wide shaded porch of the Sandpiper, where a surprisingly efficient ceiling fan kept the air moving and the mosquitoes at bay. Palms and tropical plants he couldn't identify crowded up against the white railing, as if ready to take over the old inn if given a chance. Farther off, he could hear a woodpecker tapping for his supper, and under all of it was the hypnotic lull of the ocean moving against the shore. He'd traveled the world, stayed at the most luxurious resorts in the most exotic locations, but he couldn't remember ever enjoying an evening more than he was right now.

Something about the seclusion of the location, nestled as it was against the wildlife sanctuary that made up almost half the island, allowed him to let down walls that he'd spent most of his life putting up. The friendliness of the island people was a part of it, as well. He'd wandered up and down Lighthouse Avenue, the main street through town, and every person he'd seen had greeted him openly, willing to talk about the town, their businesses and their families. He'd learned that the mayor had held office for forty years, and was running again in the spring. The streetlights came on at dusk and the shops closed soon after, but the local diner opened early for the fishermen and commuters. He'd also been warned, with a wink and a nod, that alcohol sales were banned on Sundays, so if he wanted to pick up a six-pack to watch the game with, he'd better get it today. The traditional pace of life here was worlds away from the life he'd known, but right now, sitting on a porch swing waiting for a pretty girl, it definitely had its perks.

Tires crunching over gravel signaled a car pulling into the lot hidden by thick green foliage. Leaving the sheltered sanctuary of the patio, he took the steps two at a time, then followed the winding footpath to the large gravel and sand parking lot. A bright blue compact car was in the first spot, its engine still running.

As he started toward it, the door opened, long legs swinging out. Then she stood, facing him, and he was stopped in his tracks, paralyzed. He'd remembered her as pretty, but now, in the light of day, she was stunning. Gone were the shapeless scrubs. Today she wore snug-fitting jeans and a casual but fitted navy tank top that clung to her generous curves. She'd left her hair loose, a mass of ebony curls tumbling down her back. Her striking blue eyes sparkled in the sunlight, framed by dark lashes he knew his sisters would kill for. But it was her smile, innocently seductive, that nearly knocked him over.

"Hi," she said softly, gripping the door handle. "I hope I'm not late."

"No, right on time." He forced himself back into motion, heading for the tiny car. "I heard you pull in, thought I'd save you the walk up."

"Ah, okay. Well." She started to walk toward him, then stopped. "Guess we should be going, then."

"Right, you said it fills up fast, and I'm starving. I think it's all the fresh air." He opened the car door and folded himself carefully into the seat. Although roomier than it had first appeared, it was still a tight fit for his six-foot-two frame. "Is it far?"

"Nothing's far on Paradise Isle."

"Right, I keep forgetting." He grinned. "Here on the beach, it seems the sand goes on forever. It's hard to remember that the actual town is so small."

"Most of the island is taken up by the wildlife sanctuary and public beach access. Only a small portion is actually developed." Her tone indicated that she liked things that way, and he tried not to think about how things would change if Caruso Hotels built a resort here. Instead, he focused on the view as they wound their way down the coast along the beachfront road. Pelicans dove and rose, searching for their evening meal, disappearing and reappearing from behind grass-covered dunes. Some kind of vine also grew on the dunes, with big purple flowers soaking up the evening sun.

"I didn't know flowers could grow in sand," he said, pointing to the tough-looking vines.

She smiled, either at his interest or at the flowers themselves, he wasn't sure. "That's railroad vine. They call it that because it just keeps chugging along the dune, sometimes growing a hundred feet long. The roots help hold the sand in place, protecting the dunes. Best of all, it flowers all year-round. The tall, grasslike plants around it are sea oats—not as pretty, but just as important for the dunes."

Intrigued, he had her point out a few other interesting species as they drove. By the time they reached the restaurant half a dozen names, like coco plum and wax myrtle, were spinning through his head. Impressed, he told her so.

"It's my home. To protect it, I had to learn about it," she said simply.

Another stab of guilt knifed through his stomach. At this rate, he'd be too knotted up to eat a thing. Changing the subject, he focused on the rustic, almost tumbledown appearance of Pete's Crab Shack and Burger Bar—serving the "coldest beer in town," if the worn sign above the door could be believed.

He could see what looked like a small dining area inside, but most of the patrons were sitting on the spacious, covered deck, enjoying the ocean view along with their baskets of food. Jillian led him to one of the few empty tables and passed him a plastic menu. Scanning the offerings, he quickly decided on the grilled snapper BLT, fries and a sweet tea.

"A man that knows what he wants," Jillian commented, raising her head from behind her own menu.

He met her eyes and sparks flew, hotter than the heat lightning flashing in the clouds behind her.

He knew what he wanted.

And it definitely wasn't on the menu.

Jillian felt her cheeks become flushed from the heat in Nic's eyes. Somehow, her innocent comment didn't feel so innocent anymore. Embarrassed, flattered and more than a little confused, she bit her lip and tried to think of something to say. His eyes caught the movement, narrowing on her lips. Oh, boy. Her previous casual dates had not prepared for her this level of…intensity.

Desperate to ease the tension she turned away, hoping to signal the waiter. Instead, she saw Mollie, weighed down by a giant paper sack, cutting across the deck to their table. Knowing there was no way to stop her, Jillian waved her over.

"Hey, Jillian, who's the handsome stranger?" Mollie batted her eyelashes theatrically at Nic.

"Mollie, this is Nic. He's Murphy's most recent savior. Nic, this is Mollie. She's the receptionist at the clinic, and a good friend." She gestured to the overflowing bag. "Stocking up for a hurricane?"

"Picking up dinner for Emma and me. Cassie got an emergency call, and her parents couldn't babysit, some concert or something. I said I'd swing by and pick the munchkin up, take her home and feed her. I wasn't sure what she likes, so I had Pete throw in a bit of everything." She shrugged. "I figure Cassie can eat whatever is left over when she gets home."

"An emergency? That's odd—I didn't get a call from her." Jillian dug in her purse for her phone. Cassie usually called her for assistance in emergencies.

Mollie grabbed her hand. "Chill out. She didn't call because she said you were, and I quote, 'on a hot date.'" She scanned Nic from head to toe, slowly. "I guess he qualifies." Jillian kicked her under the table. "Seriously, no worries. She said she had it handled, something about a pug having an allergic reaction. She just wants to observe it for a while at this point, make sure the medication is working."

"Oh." Somewhat appeased, she put the phone down. "Well, I'm available if she needs me."

"No, you aren't," Mollie said, winking at Nic. "Hot date, remember?" Avoiding another kick from Jillian, she took her paper bag and strolled out, obviously pleased with herself. Nic, for his part, looked incredibly amused by the entire situation.

"Something funny?"

"Nope, just enjoying myself. And the view," he added, looking pointedly at her.

Those butterflies were rapidly morphing into pterodactyls. Thankfully, Nic's flirting was curtailed by the arrival of the waitress. Jillian ordered the crab cakes, and Nic his sandwich.

The perky waitress, in shorts that covered less than most bikini bottoms, couldn't take her eyes off him, and really, who could blame her? He looked every bit as masculine and commanding in jeans and a casual button-down shirt as he had in his professional clothing the night before. If anything, the more relaxed attire highlighted his chiseled features and hard body.

Annoyed with Ms. Skimpy Pants and irritated with herself for caring, Jillian drummed her fingers on the paper placemat. Nic smiled at her frustration, but to his credit kept his eyes on her, not the scantily clad waitress, who thankfully was called away to another table.

By the time the red plastic baskets of food arrived, Jillian felt a bit more relaxed. Nic, despite his tendency to make her breath catch and pulse race, was a pleasant dining companion. They chitchatted about the weather, which was still warm, even in October, then he relayed the story of his rendezvous with the eccentric Mrs. Rosenberg. His description of her enthusiastic greeting and the way she had bamboozled him into changing her doorknob had her breathless with laughter. "I'm sorry. I should be thanking you instead of laughing at you." She shook her head. "Seriously, thanks for helping her. I'm sure she didn't give you much choice, but thanks, anyway."

"She was definitely persuasive." He sipped his tea, then continued, "But I would have done it, anyway. I'm sure she's very capable for her age, but she's not up to replacing doorknobs. And it needed to be done."

His simple answer spoke volumes about him. Most single guys didn't go around acting as handymen for little old ladies. That Nic didn't realize how uncommon his charitable streak was made it even more appealing. She found herself wanting to know more about this mystery man, and how he'd come to be so chivalrous. "Where did you learn how to change a doorknob, anyway?"

"My dad taught me. That, and a lot of other things. He didn't believe in paying someone else to do what you could do yourself. So he taught us about household repairs, car maintenance, that kind of thing."

"Us?"

"I have a brother and two sisters. I'm the oldest."

"He taught the girls to do that stuff, too?"

"Definitely. No gender discrimination there. And we all learned to cook, too, no exceptions."

"Your dad cooked?" Jillian was flabbergasted. None of her foster fathers had, of course, but most of their wives hadn't, either. She'd grown up on frozen dinners and boxed mac and cheese.

"Of course he cooked, he's Italian. But my nana is the one that taught us kids. When Mom and Dad were in the kitchen, they were busy, you know, trying to get food on the table in a hurry. Nana had more time and patience, so she taught us all. We would start with tossing salads, easy stuff, and then move up to more complicated things when we were ready. By the time we were in high school, we could all cook reasonably well." He popped a fry in his mouth. "Except for my brother, Damian. He does more than reasonably well. He just finished culinary school, and now he's in Italy getting advanced training. He's a magician with food."

"What about your sisters…what are they like?"

"Smart," he answered without hesitation. "Both are really smart, but complete opposites. Claire is a total bookworm. She's studying for a masters in English at NYU. Isabella is more practical. She has an MBA and works for a big investment firm."

His pride in them was obvious; she could tell just from his tone how much he cared for his family. A small stirring of envy clawed at her, but she pushed it away. She'd spent much of her childhood wishing for a family like his, with siblings and parents and grandparents. But she was an adult now; she'd had plenty of time to learn that wishes didn't always come true.

Nic enjoyed talking about his family, but the questions about their careers made him nervous. He knew it was dishonest, but he didn't want her to ask what his father did or what *he* did. He'd had too many women want him just because of his family, or rather the family fortune. Of course, in this case, his family being the driving force behind Caruso Hotels didn't seem like news she'd be happy to hear, with the Sandpiper being up for sale. If she knew he was here to look into buying it, well, that would definitely wipe the smile off her face.

And it was a knockout of a smile. Her whole face glowed, and her nose scrunched up, just a little, in the most adorable way. In the end, business would have to stay business. His father and the whole company were counting on him to make this deal. If he was going to take over from his dad one day, he needed to prove he could handle the job. But in the meantime, he couldn't help but want to spend some time with a woman who seemed to like him, not his money or his glamorous lifestyle.

Hoping to change the subject, he asked casually, "So what about your family? Do they live around here?" Her face blanched, just briefly, and he saw a flash of pain in her eyes that had him reaching for her hand as she caught her breath. Caught off guard by her reaction, he kept silent as he waited.

She looked down at their joined hands, then into his eyes.

"I don't have any family."

When he didn't react, other than to squeeze her hand reassuringly, she continued. "My parents died in a car accident when I was two years old. They were caught in a bad storm and lost control of the car. I'm told they died on impact, but paramedics found me buckled in my car seat, not a scratch on me."

He didn't know what to say, had nothing to offer, other than "I'm sorry."

Smiling at that, she said, "Yeah, so am I. They—I— didn't have any family, at least that anyone knew of. I ended up in foster care, moving every year or so. Eventually I ended up here, on Paradise Isle. When I was in high school, I got an after-school job at the clinic, back when Cassie's dad was still running things. Later, when my foster parents moved to Jacksonville, I convinced the social worker to let me stay here. I had some money saved up, and I got some financial assistance from the state. I finished out my senior year living in a motel room. After I graduated and could work full-time, I found an apartment and started classes at the community college. A few years ago, I passed my State Board exams, and got certified as a veterinary technician."

"You've been on your own since high school? With no help?"

"I had my friends, and Doc Marshall, Cassie's father, helped by convincing the case worker not to put me back in foster care. I was almost eighteen and with foster homes so scarce, it wasn't a hard sell. But without him backing me, and giving me a job, it never would have worked."

Nic couldn't even imagine that kind of self-reliance. His family had always been involved in his life—sometimes too involved. But as much as their expectations and demands could feel like an albatross around his neck, they had always been there for him when he needed them. They were the only people he could truly count on.

No wonder Jillian was so attached to the community—it was all she had. The guilt he had pushed aside began chewing a fresh hole in his gut. If he green-lighted the Caruso Hotel project, it would completely change the island, and although he'd assumed that change would be for the better, he had a feeling she wouldn't agree.

Carefully, he tried to feel her out on the subject. "So why Paradise? Of everywhere you lived, what made you stay here?"

Jillian smiled. "Because it felt like home. Nowhere

else ever did. Here, the people I met really seemed to care, to want to know me. No one brushed me off as just a foster kid, or acted like I was a lost cause. The town is small enough that people really get to know each other—there are no strangers. And everyone looks out for each other. It's the closest I've ever come to having family." Her voice quavered at her last few words, leaving no doubt as to the extent of her loyalty.

Nic wanted to argue, to offer some counterpoint, but he couldn't. Even in his short time on the island, he'd seen the camaraderie she was describing. Her friend Mollie's willingness to give up her Saturday night to help a friend was just one more example. He wished he could say there were plenty of places like Paradise, but if there were, he'd never seen them.

Of course, small towns, isolated from the fast pace of modern life, weren't his usual haunts. Caruso Hotels were found in the busier tourist destinations; some of their larger resorts became cities unto themselves. On paper, Paradise Isle had seemed like a blank canvas, waiting for development. Choosing an unknown place wasn't their usual mode of operation, but he'd thought it a brilliant and cost-saving strategy, one that would pay handsomely when they transformed Paradise Isle into a tourist hot spot.

Now, seeing the town for himself, he realized how arrogant he'd been. Paradise might be small, but that didn't mean it was insignificant. A revelation that was a bit too late in coming. How could he tell his father, the CEO of a world-renowned business, not to purchase a prime piece of property because "the people are really nice"? It was absurd. He'd just have to figure something out.

And find a way to live with himself afterward.

* * *

Jillian hadn't meant to go on and on about her childhood; she hated it when people felt sorry for her. But Nic didn't look as if he pitied her. If anything, he looked thoughtful as she talked about Paradise, her adopted hometown. She found herself wondering what his hometown was like, but before she could ask he was signaling the waitress for the check. "No, I'm buying," she protested. "We agreed. I'm treating you, to thank you for being Murphy's knight in shining armor. And for helping Mrs. Rosenberg. "

"I changed my mind." He handed his credit card to the waitress without even looking at the check. "What kind of knight lets the princess foot the bill? Besides, I'm the one who should be grateful. You stayed late to help a stranger—"

"Murphy isn't a stranger—" she objected.

"No, but I was. And you didn't know it was Murphy when you let me in. And you've kept me from eating alone or worse, falling prey to our waitress over there." The woman in question was still making eyes at him, none too subtly.

"A fate worse than death," she teased. "Better watch out, she's headed our way."

He just grinned, and signed the offered receipt without taking his eyes off Jillian. The waitress, realizing she was being ignored, practically stomped off. *Not so perky anymore*, Jillian thought, more pleased than she had a right to be.

She knew she had no claim on this gorgeous man, but she was enjoying his company, and the way he made her feel. He listened to her, really listened, and when he spoke, he was funny and engaging. And of course, he wasn't exactly hard on the eyes. Several times she had embarrassed herself by staring at him; thankfully he didn't seem to have noticed. She'd never been so quick to be attracted to a man before, but Nic had intrigued her from the first minute she'd seen him.

When he took her elbow to guide her down the steep stairs she didn't object, nor did she protest when he opened her car door for her after she unlocked it with the remote. His actions were quaintly old-fashioned, and that appealed to her more than she would have expected.

She turned on the air conditioner as soon as she got in, hoping to relieve the oven-like temperature, zooming the windows down to let some of the hot air escape. Once on the road, she put them back up, cocooning them in a car that suddenly seemed quite claustrophobic. His scent permeated the air, some kind of aftershave or cologne that smelled clean yet spicy.

As she merged onto the main road, he reached over and rested a broad hand on hers where it gripped the gearshift. An innocent touch, but it had her pulse racing. All at once the drive to the Sandpiper felt too long and yet not long enough. She was still debating how to handle things when she pulled into the Sandpiper's secluded parking lot.

Should she take her hand back? Kiss him? Let him kiss her? Or maybe she was misreading the whole thing, and the attraction was completely one-sided.

Confused, she turned to find him watching her, searing her skin with his gaze. Energy was radiating off him in waves. Frozen, she could only blink as he reached to brush a lock of hair from her face, twirling it around one finger. They both seemed to hold their breath as he gently tugged, then untwined it curl by curl.

She moistened her lips, and he shifted his attention to her mouth. Sensuously, he traced a finger over the swollen nerve endings, the sensation causing her eyes to flutter closed. There was a whisper of air as he leaned toward her, and then his mouth was on hers.

His kiss was gentle at first, a request, not a demand. But when her lips parted on a sigh he accepted the invitation, deepening the kiss. As his tongue teased, she reached for him blindly, finding his broad shoulders, clutching him to her, not wanting him to stop, not able to stop. Never had she experienced a connection like this. This was so far beyond a kiss; it was some kind of magic, and she never wanted it to end. Straining toward him, but trapped by the seat belt, she whimpered in frustration.

Immediately he let her go, backing away to his side of the car. "Did I hurt you?" His worried eyes darted over her, obviously mistaking her whimper for a sign of pain.

"No," she managed, her voice shaky. "No, that definitely didn't hurt." Finding her composure, and realizing he really was concerned, she explained, "The seat belt was in my way."

"Oh."

She could see now that he was breathing as hard as she was. So she had affected him, too. A bit of feminine pride crept over her.

"Tomorrow. What are your plans tomorrow?" His tone was insistent, compelling her to respond.

"Um...I usually go to church in the morning, the early service, but otherwise, I'm not sure. I don't really have any." Until now, painting her nails and catching up on reality TV were generally the highlights of her weekend.

"Spend the day with me." When she hesitated, he pushed. "Show me your island, give me the grand tour."

She considered. She certainly wanted to spend more time with him, and it was an innocent enough request. But this man was trouble wrapped up in sin. If he could get her this worked up over dinner and a short car ride, who knows what would happen with a full day together? He knocked down walls she didn't even know she had, and she wasn't sure she was ready for that.

As if sensing her hesitation, he withdrew as far as he could in the small confines of the car and said, "I'll be a perfect gentleman, I swear."

He really was cute. Giving in, she nodded. "All right, what time do you want me to pick you up?"

"How about ten thirty? And no offense, but I'd rather we take my rental. More legroom."

He had a point; he barely fit in her little compact. But she knew enough about basic safety to avoid giving out her address to a man she barely knew. "Let's meet at The Grind, a coffee shop on Lighthouse Avenue, a few blocks from the clinic. They've got great coffee, and they carry pastries from the local bakery if you want something sweet."

"I think I just had something sweet."

She felt her cheeks heating again at his casual innuendo. Flashing her a very male, very satisfied smile, he let himself out of the car. She watched him walk confidently toward the inn, as if he hadn't completely rocked her world.

Dear heavens, what on earth did she just get herself into?

Chapter Five

The cool dimness of the All Saints sanctuary never failed to soothe Jillian. The scent of incense clinging to the walls and the flicker of dripping candles made her feel as if she'd stepped out of the ordinary world, and into someplace timeless.

Most of the old wooden pews were empty this early in the morning—the eleven-o'clock service was much more popular. Which was the main reason she avoided it. Seeing all those happy families squeezed into the pews, children whispering, parents trying to keep them quiet, made her ache for what she had missed out on. So she came early, and then had the rest of the day for errands and chores.

Today, the stillness of the old building was particularly welcome. She'd had a restless, sleepless night, tossing and turning while reliving Nic's kiss. Of course, now, in the light of day, she felt silly getting so worked up over a single kiss.

As she prayed, waiting for the service to start, she felt the bench shift, signaling that someone had joined her in the pew. Her peripheral vision caught the familiar motions of the sign of the cross. Finished with her own prayers, she eased back into her seat and turned to greet her pew mate. *Nic?* "What are you doing here?" she whispered.

"Praying?" he whispered back, all innocence.

"No, seriously, what you are doing here? Are you some kind of stalker or something?"

"What, I can't just be here for my own redemption? Remember, big Italian family, church attendance comes with the territory." At her narrowed brows, he admitted, "Okay, so I'm not going to win any attendance awards. But I did grow up in the church, was an altar boy and everything."

She tried, but could not picture this wickedly sexy man as an altar boy. He might have been an innocent child once, but you'd never know it now. When she continued to glare at him, he confessed, "I talked to my mom on the phone last night, and it came up that I was meeting you after church. I thought I would score big points by saying I met a nice girl." He rubbed his neck ruefully. "But she just wanted to know why I wasn't going to church, too. By the time I got off the phone I had promised I'd go, and that I'd say a prayer for Aunt Irene's cataract surgery."

Jillian stifled a chuckle, aware that their conversation was starting to draw attention. Nic might be a grown man, but he obviously still respected his mother. Definite bonus points. "So, did you pray for Aunt Irene yet?"

His answer was cut off by the processional hymn. Standing, she stood shoulder to shoulder with him, his masculine presence impossible to ignore. He held out his hymnal for her to share, and although she appreciated the gesture she was flustered enough to stumble over the words more than once. He had no such issue, his rich baritone voice carrying the notes clearly. She was still feeling unsettled when they sat to listen to the readings, but eventually was carried away by the familiar readings, songs and worship. By the end of the service she found she was actually enjoying his company, and told him so as they filed out into the sunlight.

"Sorry I acted so startled in there. I'm not used to having company in church, but it was nice."

"How long have you been going here? It seemed everyone in there knew you by name."

"Most of them do. When I turned eighteen, my case worker gave me a packet with all my information in it, including my baptism certificate. I was so young when my parents died, I don't have any real memories of them, but I do know that my mom attended church, and that religion was important enough to her to have me baptized. Saying the prayers she said, singing the hymns she sang, it makes me feel closer to her somehow." She stopped, wary of oversharing. "That probably sounds silly."

"Not silly. It makes perfect sense. I'm sure she'd be very proud of you." He stopped, looked at his watch. "So we have most of the day left to play. Do you still want to hit the coffee shop? Or something else?"

She squinted at him; the bright sun overhead had already heated things up considerably. She sized him up and made a decision. "You go get the coffee, and I'll meet you there—I just need to run home first. Cream and sugar, please. Oh, and pick out some muffins or scones or something." She paused. "And get a couple of bottles of water. You're going to need them." Then she walked off before he could ask any more questions. This time, she was in charge, and she liked it that way.

Nic had no idea what Jillian was planning, but he might as well go with the flow. Tomorrow he had to meet with a city council member to discuss infrastructure plans, look into possible traffic and utilities issues, and then write up his findings before getting on a cross-country flight to Las Vegas. So today, he was going to enjoy himself as much as possible. He'd promised himself that much. Everyone and everything else could wait.

He stretched out his legs beneath the small sidewalk table outside the coffee shop. The sun was hot enough that he had chosen khaki shorts and a golf shirt instead of slacks this morning, deciding that was dressy enough for church, given the steamy weather. As he sipped from the eco-friendly paper cup he watched the Sunday morning street life ebb and flow around him. Children with dripping ice cream cones and sticky smiles, parents with shopping bags or grocery lists, all smiled or nodded a greeting to him as they passed. From his shaded vantage point under The Grind's awning he could see quite a bit of Lighthouse Avenue.

Across from him was the Sugar Cone, an old-fashioned ice cream parlor. Treasures of the Sea, a gift shop of some kind, abutted it on one side, and a used bookstore called Beach Reads was on the other. On his side of the street, there was a pharmacy to his left, and beyond that Framed, which looked to be some kind of art gallery and photo studio. To his right was a bicycle shop, and farther down were restaurants, a grocer and a clothing boutique.

On his drive over he had also passed a post office, medical clinic and the hardware store. There were no big box stores on the island, no shopping malls or dance clubs. There was one bar, more tavern than nightclub, over on the beach side, near Pete's, but there was not much in the way of nightlife. That would mean that a Caruso Hotel built here would need an on-site nightclub to satisfy its usual customer base. Recognizing he was still in work mode, he gave himself a mental shake. Surely he could spend one day focused on pleasure, not business.

Recommitted to that goal, he munched on one of the donuts he'd picked out and went back to soaking up the beach town ambiance.

Spotting a woman approaching, he blinked in surprise. Was that Jillian? She'd changed into tight athletic shorts, a spaghetti-strap tank top the color of daisies, and had her hair pulled through the hole in a white ball cap. Struggling a bit, she was pushing a metallic-green bike with oversize tires.

"What is that?" he asked, pointing to the odd-looking bike.

"It's a fat bike, for riding on sand. And it's yours, for the day, anyway. Here—" she shoved the bike at him "—hold this, I'll be right back with mine."

Bemused, he propped the bike against a pillar and waited while she went back into the bike shop. She soon came out with a similar, if slightly smaller, blue version of the first bike. Leaning it with his, she plopped down in the seat across from him and snatched one of the donuts. "Those are easier to ride than push," she commented, before taking a large bite of the sticky confection.

"I certainly hope so. It's been a while since I've ridden a bike, other than the stationary one at the gym."

"Well, you know what they say—you never forget how." She tasted the coffee next, and he got to see her eyes close in a look of pure bliss. "Best coffee on the island."

"So what's the plan?" He eyed the bike uncertainly. He hoped she was right about not forgetting how to ride. The last real bike he'd ridden had been a ten-speed in junior high. And that had been on pavement, not sand.

"First, I'm going to eat another donut and finish this coffee. Then sunscreen—don't make that face, because the sun's brutal here and even tough guys wear sunscreen—then we bike down the avenue, and take Palmetto. That's the way you would have come in on, over to the coast road. We'll take the ramp down to the beach and ride all the way to the Sandpiper." She grinned. "If you're a good boy, we'll stop for lunch along the way."

"Oh, I'm very, very good," he responded, rising to the bait. While she finished the last donut he disposed of the trash and secured a water bottle to each bike. He noticed she had an insulated bag attached to the rear rack of her bike, and wondered what other surprises she had in store.

He'd wanted something different, something outside of his normal routine, and he was getting exactly that. He even let her mount and ride ahead of him—although it chafed his ego a bit—since she was the one giving the tour.

"Follow me, watch for pedestrians and holler if you need to stop," she called over her shoulder, merging into the meager Sunday traffic.

He immediately realized there was a definite upside

to taking up the rear position. Namely, the good view he had of her rear end. Shapely and athletic, it was more than enough to take his mind off his rusty biking abilities. Watching her ride, her black curls blowing in the wind, firm legs pumping up and down, he was so distracted that they had ridden several blocks before he remembered he was supposed to be taking in the scenery. Forcing himself to look away, he made himself notice the tidy storefronts as they continued down Lighthouse Avenue. He'd seen only one franchise business, and that was a gas station. All the other stores were obviously run and owned by locals, and seemed to be thriving despite any problems in the larger economy.

Paradise Isle might be a small town, but it certainly was flourishing. Not having a direct connection to I-95 had kept it isolated, but the town didn't seem to be hurting from the lack of exposure. As they turned into a more residential area, passing picturesque Spanish-style stucco homes alongside the small wooden "shotgun"-style cottages, he couldn't help feel that the people he saw mowing lawns and walking dogs were not going to be eager to have the floodgates of Florida tourism thrown open. Normally that wasn't something that he would even think about. But now, every time Jillian turned back to smile at him, he felt his sense of duty pulling him down like a weight, one he didn't know how to escape.

By the time they reached the beach, Jillian was sweating, but exuberant. The sight of the ocean, as common as it was to an islander, never failed to thrill her. Nic had been a great biking companion, staying far enough behind for safety, but close enough to hear if she needed to give directions. Not that she had doubted his athleticism, not with that body.

Stopping to rest under the shade of the sea grapes that grew around the access ramps, she freed her water bottle from its rack and drank her fill. Nic did the same, his head tilted back, tanned skin gleaming with sweat as he gulped the cool water. Watching, Jillian's mouth went dry. She raised her own bottle again to cover her slack-jawed staring.

He finished drinking and looked around. "This was a great idea—definitely more fun than the bike at the gym."

"Not much of a compliment, but I'm glad you're enjoying it. But before you get too enthusiastic, remember, we still have the beach ride."

"I'm game if you are." Daring her, he pushed off and started down the beach, leaving Jillian to catch up. She laughed out loud, and stood on the pedals to get more speed. When they hit the hard-packed sand near the water, he paralleled the coast and slowed for her to catch him. Nodding, acknowledging his win, she pulled abreast and set a more leisurely, and safer, pace down the fairly crowded beach.

Just like every other weekend there were bronzed teenagers, slick with suntan lotion showing off for their friends, eager children digging in the sand while their parents watched, and surfers on colorful boards fighting for the perfect wave. But even as everything looked the same, it felt different. She felt different. She felt…happy.

Being with Nic made her happy in a way that nothing else ever had. There was a warmth deep inside that was filling her up, as if the sun's rays were somehow penetrating all the way to her heart. In such a short time this one person had filled a hole in her life, in her heart, that she had spent years trying to ignore.

But as wonderful as he made her feel, she was scared to death of what that feeling meant, and what would happen when he left town. She'd lost her heart too many times in her life to be willing to risk that kind of pain again. Her parents, foster parents, foster siblings…they had all left, and she had the emotional scars to prove it. Sure, someday she wanted a family of her own, but getting attached to a tourist was a bad bet. Of course, that didn't mean they couldn't have a good time today, enjoy some food and activity, and then part as fond acquaintances, if not friends.

Resolved, she turned and smiled, shoving down the tingling that shot through her when he grinned back, boyish enthusiasm lighting up his face. Unlike a lot of the guys she had dated, he had nothing to prove, and was secure enough to be silly and have fun without worrying he'd look less manly. A refreshing change, one that made it hard to keep her guard up.

They cruised along, eventually leaving the populated part of the beach for the deserted stretch between the public access area and the Sandpiper. Awed, as always, by the pristine beauty, she slowed her pace to take it all in. White sand stretched for miles in either direction, marred only by the tracks of the industrious little sandpipers the nearby inn was named for. Even the ocean was at peace here, swelling slowly and stretching to the shore in a smooth arc, rather than crashing and foaming against the beach.

Signaling to Nic, she slowed, and then stopped. "I'm ready for a break, if that's okay with you."

He wiped the sweat from his forehead and ran a

hand through his damp hair, his fingers mussing the dark waves. "Sure, you're the boss." He drank from his water bottle and looked around at her chosen resting point. "This is amazing. I've been on beaches all over the world, but this is something else. I feel like we're on a deserted island. I can't believe how close this is to the main part of town. It feels so far away."

"I know. It's amazing to have something this pristine only a bike ride from home. And the Sandpiper is only a little ways around that bend. They don't get busy enough to disturb this part of the beach." Sitting down on the sand, she removed her tennis shoes, stuffing her socks into them. "Come on. Let's get our feet wet, cool off a bit."

After a moment's hesitation, Nic followed suit, toeing off his boat shoes and following her to the ocean's edge. The water was perfect, just cool enough to be refreshing but not cold. "Wow, that feels amazing."

She walked a little ways down the shore, splashing like a kid. There was nothing better than sun, sand and surf to clear the mind. Nic strolled with her, gradually easing closer. Trapped, she couldn't move away from him without getting into deeper water.

When he took her hand, she knew she should say something, remind him that they were just friends. But her voice caught in her throat, and she reveled in the touch of his warm, calloused palm, swinging their arms as they walked.

She was so focused on that point of contact that it took her several moments to realize how far they had strayed from the bikes. Stopping, her hand tugged on his, turning him to her. She wanted to tell him that they should go back, but his eyes locked on hers, and the words wouldn't form. He used their linked hands to pull her toward him, close against his chest. His left hand was still tangled in hers; he buried his other in her hair, anchoring her as she stood in the swirling water. She felt her heart tumble as if buffeted by the waves around him, all of her arguments washed out to sea. Logically, this was a bad idea, but she had left her good sense on the beach with the bikes and their shoes. Instead of pulling away, she arched up to him, ready to meet his kiss.

Splash!

Sprayed with water from head to toe, Jillian jolted, stepping back as far as his grip on her hair would let her.

"What the heck?" Nic let her go and wiped the salty water from his eyes. "What on earth just happened? Is this some kind of practical joke?"

"A pelican." Jillian, now free, retreated another step. She shook her head at the dumb luck of it. "He was diving for a fish. Usually they don't come so close to people, but a few get enough handouts from fishermen to make them pretty bold. I've never been quite that close, though." Heart pounding from the near miss with the bird, and the even nearer miss with Nic, she headed for the bikes, her steps quick and precise. She was going to have to be much more careful from now on, if she wanted to keep her pride, and her heart, intact.

After the pelican's untimely interruption, Nic found straddling a bike to be a tricky business. Luckily, his baggy shorts camouflaged the extent of his response. But discomfort aside, it was best they move on, putting the near kiss behind them. He was leaving tomorrow, and when he came back, if he came back, it would be to buy the inn she was so desperate to save. Under those circumstances, kissing her, sleeping with her, would be unethical. He had been raised better than that.

He'd never lied to a woman to get her into bed; hell, he'd never needed to. Not once they found out he was an heir to the Caruso fortune. And although he hadn't exactly lied to Jillian, he wasn't being honest, either.

There was no way around it—she and that hot body of hers were off-limits. Not that she was chasing him down; she'd all but run once he'd let her go. Something he should be grateful for.

"The Sandpiper's just ahead. We'll have lunch there on the back deck, if that's okay." Jillian pedaled easily alongside him, as if nothing had happened. Fine, if she wasn't going to bring up their near kiss, he certainly wasn't going to.

"Sounds good to me." He figured they'd order in or get something from the small kitchen at the inn, but when they parked their bikes, she unstrapped the insulated bag from hers, tossing it to him.

"Lunch is served."

Intrigued, he carried the bag up the stairs to the wide, covered deck of the Sandpiper. Shaded by an upper-level balcony and boasting several paddle fans, it was at least ten degrees cooler than the beach below. Cushioned lounge chairs at one end and an outdoor dining area at the other looked out over the water below.

He set the bag on the table and started fishing out the contents. Instead of the typical sandwich and chips, he found several plastic containers filled with obviously homemade food, as well as a small loaf of crusty bread and a thermos of lemonade. "This looks a lot better than the soggy peanut butter and jelly sandwiches I remember from picnics as a kid." He held up one of the containers. "What is all this stuff?"

"The smaller container is a smoked fish spread, made with locally caught amberjack. There are crackers to go with it. Then those two have salads in them, greens with cold chicken and a citrus dressing. And that last one has a couple of slices of key lime pie in it." She opened the smoked fish and spread some on a cracker for him. "Try it, it's good stuff."

Starving, Nic shoved the cracker in his mouth. Smoky and sweet, the flavors exploded across his taste buds. "Wow...that's seriously good," he managed to get out around the mouthful of food. "I wonder if I can buy this stuff at home." Not that he was ever home long enough to bother grocery shopping. Ignoring that depressing thought, he reached for the dish and began loading up another cracker.

Jillian sorted out the rest of the food, and he eagerly accepted his share of salad, a hunk of the crusty bread and a paper cup of lemonade. Chewing, he ate in silence, determined to keep his eyes on the view of the ocean and not on the way her shirt, damp now from the pelican encounter, clung enticingly to curves he wasn't supposed to notice. A losing battle if there ever was one.

"Penny for your thoughts."

Had she seen him staring? She was chasing a piece of lettuce with her fork, and didn't seem upset, so maybe not. "Just thinking how impressive the view is." And not just of the beach.

"It is. It's been a while since I've sat back here." Her eyes went soft, as if she was seeing something he couldn't. "Lots of memories here."

"You've stayed at the Sandpiper?"

"As a guest? No. But before the last owners died, they would host all sorts of community events. Fish fries to raise money for the fire department, Fourth of July fireworks displays, a big Christmas tree lighting party, that kind of thing. The place was pretty much the heart of the island for decades. Toward the end they were too frail to run things the way they wanted to, and when their daughter inherited, she was too busy for that sort of thing." Her mouth curved into a small smile. "Some of us are hoping to get it listed on the register of historical places. That would mean grant money, which would allow the city to buy it when it goes up for sale. I'd love to see it back in the center of things."

She paused, as if weighing if she should continue. "The thing is, when I was a kid and came here alone, everyone else was with their families. I'd always hoped to bring my own family here one day. So I offered to write the grant proposal myself. Saving the Sandpiper would be a way to hold on to that childhood dream."

The creamy pie turned bitter in his mouth. The hope in her eyes tore at him. The better part of him wanted to respond to that innocent dream, to help her achieve what she so obviously wanted. But it was impossible. His duty was to his family, to his company, not to this siren of an orphan, no matter what spell she had cast on him.

So he would do his damn job, do what he had to do. But that didn't mean he had to keep lying to her about it. He'd just have to find a way to explain things. Even if it made her hate him.

Chapter Six

Nic had been quiet ever since their picnic at the Sand-piper. He'd definitely seemed distracted on the bike ride back into town; she hoped he wasn't still upset about the kiss. Correction, the nonkiss. She'd been about to jump into his arms, and then had practically run away. Talk about mixed signals. Not something he usually dealt with, she was sure. He probably had his pick of women back home, wherever that was. She needed to get him talking about where he was from, to remind her brain that he was just a temporary distraction. Maybe then the weird tingling sensation running through her body would go away.

"So, where are you from, anyway? You never really said." Watching him out of the corner of her eye, she baited her hook with a piece of squid and executed a near perfect cast over the pier's guardrail. Fishing at the Paradise Isle Pier was a favorite way to relax, and something she'd wanted to share with him, ridiculous as that was. She really knew so little about him, other than that he wore expensive suits, cared for stray dogs and old ladies, and was way better looking than any man had a right to be.

"I'm from New Jersey, at least originally. I've got a place in Manhattan now, but I still don't think of it as home."

"You don't like New York?"

"I like it fine. You know, it's true what they say—it is the city that never sleeps. There is always something to do—anytime, day or night. I just never seem to find the time to actually do any of those things." He rubbed the stubble on his face, as if just noticing it. "I work a lot. Pretty much all the time. Spending a day like this, just enjoying myself, going with the flow... I can't remember the last time I did that." He cast his line out almost as well as she had her own. "It's a curse for a lot of us in the city. We move there for the culture, the plays, the museums, the nightclubs, and then work so damned hard we never actually see any of it."

"That sounds awful." She worked hard to support herself, but even back when she was taking classes at night and working days at the clinic, she'd always had time for walks on the beach, or a few hours fishing on the weekend.

"I shouldn't complain. I do well for myself, and a lot of people would kill for my job. And it's not like I'm working every day. But I'm out of town more than I'm home, and the rare times I am there and have a day off, I feel like I need to spend it with my family." He turned to her, earnestness shining in his eyes. "I realize I probably sound like a jerk, complaining about family, when I should just realize how lucky I am to have them. But I don't mean it like that. I love my family, and I love spending time with them. It's just…"

"Overwhelming?"

He flinched at her word choice. "That's pretty terrible, isn't it?"

Was that shame she saw in his eyes? She put a hand on his arm. "No, I think I understand. You want to be there for them, but you want a life that's your own, too." She'd always romanticized the idea of big families, but maybe it wasn't always picture-perfect.

"Right. I just feel like I have so much responsibility at work, so many people counting on me, and then there's my family, counting on me, as well. Keeping everyone happy is a nearly impossible job." He turned back to the water, watching his line with more intensity than it probably warranted.

Sensing he was uncomfortable revealing so much, she kept her tone casual, her eyes on the water. "Wanting your own life, your own destiny, that isn't terrible. You just need to find a way to do it."

"It's not that simple." He tugged hard at his line, reeling it in and then whipping it back out.

"Why not?" She stopped pretending to watch the water, and faced him head-on. "Why can't you work less, or just tell your boss you need more time off?"

"Because I work for my family. It's a family business. If I don't get the job done, I'm not just slacking on the job, I'm betraying my family." The muscles around his eyes were tense, his jaw hard. "My parents raised me to believe that family comes first. Loyalty matters. My dad always wanted me to take over one day, or at least play a significant role in the company. He started it from scratch and built something he could be proud of. I need to live up to that. I won't let him down. I owe him."

"Wow. Okay, that does complicate things." She was in over her head here; she had no experience balancing family and work, let alone managing them both together. But it was easy to see that he was both intensely loyal and proud. With no advice to give, she was better off just listening. "So what kind of business is it, anyway?"

Nic set his pole into one of the holders screwed into the railing, and faced her, shoulders squared as if preparing for a blow. "Hotels. My family owns Caruso Hotels."

"But…" She tried to think, get her bearings. Caruso Hotels? They were one of the biggest hotel chains in the country, catering to high-end tourists. There was even one opening in Orlando soon. She'd read something about it in the paper, and from the sketches it had included, it was going to be a world-class resort. "The Caruso Hotels? The ones with the fancy resorts all over the East Coast?"

"We're expanding out West, too. I'm flying to Vegas tomorrow to handle some issues with a land deal out there." His voice betrayed not a single shred of emotion.

"Wait—land deal?" Her heart sunk. Bits and pieces of their conversations coalesced, forming a picture she didn't want to see. She had to physically force the question past the lump in her throat. "What exactly is it you do for Caruso Hotels?"

"I'm Vice President in Charge of Acquisitions." He hesitated.

"Go ahead, tell me." She wasn't letting him get away with anything less than the whole truth, late though it was.

"I scout out new locations for our hotels, negotiate sales and make sure the building process goes smoothly."

"So you aren't just here on vacation, are you?" she accused, the words like acid in her mouth.

"To be fair, I never said I was." His denial was too little, too late. As if he realized it, he continued. "I came here to check out a potential new location, a property that recently came up for sale."

Her stomach clenched; she knew what he was going to say, but she had to hear him say it. Fisting her hands, she asked, "What location? What property are you looking to buy?"

"The Sandpiper." She rocked back as if he'd hit her. He was here to buy the Sandpiper? The city didn't stand a chance against a corporate giant like Caruso Hotels. At least now she knew why he'd been wearing a designer suit when they had first met; he'd probably been wheeling and dealing all day. And now he was here to do the same.

She'd trusted him. Told him about her childhood, her dreams for the future. And all the while he'd been planning to crush those dreams like so much sand beneath his feet. How stupid was she, to imagine he felt something for her? Here she was, thinking how he was the first man to make her heart beat faster, and he'd just been looking to get the inside scoop on the island.

Tears stung her eyes, but she refused to let them fall. "So today was just another day on the job for you, huh? Market research or whatever?" She swiped at her face. "So glad I could be of service."

Hurt flashed in his eyes before he composed his features. As if he had the right to be hurt. She was the victim, not him. "What, can't stand the truth?"

"Today wasn't about business. Hell, it's probably the first day I've had in almost a year that I didn't work." He shook his head, pacing the pier. "I have meetings scheduled for tomorrow, but this weekend was supposed to be an attempt at some downtime. Maybe try on the idea of a personal life for once. You were a part of that. This place was part of that."

"Right. Well, excuse me for thinking that a tour of the island's best tourist spots might be of professional interest to someone intent on exploiting the town for his financial gain. I might not have been part of the original plan, but hey, sometimes you just get lucky."

"Seriously? I don't want to exploit anyone. I'm just trying to do my damn job. People are counting on me. My family is counting on me."

"Right, it's all about family. How could a poor little orphan understand something like that? Obviously, I have no idea what it's like to care about people." The anger and the pain tangled within her. How could she have been so naive? How could he have been so deceitful?

"That isn't what I meant. None of this is what I meant, what I wanted to happen." He reached out toward her, grasping her arm. "You have to believe me."

Locking down her heart, she shook him off. "Tell it to the fish. Maybe they'll believe it."

Nic watched her storm off, mired in guilt. He'd totally screwed up. Yes, his hands were tied, but that didn't justify the way he'd hurt her. And he had hurt her; he could see the pain shimmering just beneath her anger. He didn't blame her; he'd behaved badly. But it *was* business.

He should let her go before he made things worse. Just move on, get back to work and do what needed to be done, like always. Somehow, though, that didn't feel right. He had gotten this far in life by going with his gut, and right now his gut said he needed to make this right. Not because he thought he had a chance with her—he knew that was out of the question—but because, business or not, she'd gotten to him. The whole damned place had gotten to him.

Mind made up, he started after her. His own stride was twice the length of hers, and he was able to catch up before she was even halfway down the long wood-and-stone pier. "Hey, wait."

"No." She quickened her pace.

"Let me make it up to you."

"What? Now you want to bribe me? Maybe that works in New York City, but here we put people before profit. I don't want your money." Her shoulders shook. "I don't want anything from you."

"What if I help you with the grant?"

"What?" She stopped, faced him, eyes wide, brows raised.

Uh-oh, where had that idea come from?

Not one to go back on his word, he scrambled for mental traction. "Well, I could help you write the grant. If you get it, I'll back off, let the city buy the property."

"Why would you do that?" Her steady stare bored into him, daring him to lie.

"Because if the Sandpiper is listed as a historical site, it could mean a legal battle when we tear it down." Which was true.

They had the legal means to fight any challenges, but the press would be ugly, making it a huge hassle none of the executives would want to deal with. Of course, they also wouldn't want him to help write the grant proposal, but that didn't matter right now. "Listen, I've got some connections, and a lot of background dealing with properties of various importance. I'll help you however I can, and if the grant goes through I'll find somewhere else to build."

"And if it doesn't?"

"Then Caruso Hotels will make an offer." He wasn't going to lie. He was already kicking himself for his earlier misrepresentation. He'd always been a man of his word, and any hint of dishonor disgusted him. For his own sake, as well as hers, he wanted to make it up to her, and to do that they had to trust each other.

Appearing to consider his offer, she bit her plump bottom lip, forcing him to look away before he forgot this was about business, not pleasure. Thankfully, even if she took him up on his offer, they'd be collaborating long-distance; he obviously had control issues when it came to her.

"How would you even do this? You're leaving for where? Reno? The application process isn't something that can be done in one night."

"Vegas, and no, I'm not planning to do this tonight." In fact, he planned to stay far, far away from her tonight. "I work on the road all the time. Between video conferencing and email, we should be able to get it done without any real face-to-face contact." He should be relieved that there would be so much distance between them, but instead an odd heaviness settled in his bones. He drew a deep breath, suddenly exhausted. "I'll leave my contact info with the Sandpiper before I go. Just email me the forms and I'll take a look at what we're dealing with."

Shading her eyes against the setting sun, head cocked, she asked, "Who *are* you?"

"I thought we just covered that. Nic—technically, Dominic—Caruso. Do you want to see my identification or something?"

"No, I mean, I don't know. I just don't get it. One minute you're saving puppies, then helping old ladies, and now you are going to help me try to save the property you came here to buy. I don't understand. Why are you doing all this?"

"Honestly? I have no idea."

Chapter Seven

Nic was still trying to understand his own motives when he got back to his room that evening. Yes, he'd felt guilty about withholding his true intentions from Jillian, but that wasn't enough to explain his impulsive, and honestly reckless, offer to help her. The last thing he needed was another person looking at him to fix everything; he got enough of that from his job. And yet here he was, taking on exactly that. Maybe he was just a masochist. What other explanation was there? Sure, he was attracted to her, but attractive women weren't exactly in short supply. So why was he willing to risk a business deal for one? Maybe it was because, unlike his family or the women he tended to date, she didn't have any preconceived expectations of him? She'd certainly been shocked when he offered to help.

Pushing away his muddled thoughts, he entered the

room and absently noted that it had been tidied and the bedcovers turned down. After tossing down his wallet and keys on the nightstand, he headed straight for the shower, where a stack of clean white towels awaited him. He certainly couldn't fault the service at the Sandpiper, or much else about it, for that matter.

He turned the shower knob to hot and stripped down. When the temperature was sufficiently close to scalding, he stepped in, letting the water pound his knotted muscles. High-stakes deals, red-tape snarls and near constant travel made tension his normal condition, and he'd long ago found that a hot shower did more to relieve the stress than a bottle of whiskey. Of course, the whiskey was more fun, but with meetings back-to-back tomorrow, he couldn't afford the hangover.

He braced his hands on the cool tile and lowered his head, letting his mind wander as the jets of water worked their magic on his neck and back. Behind his closed eyelids he saw Jillian again, how she'd looked at the pier with the setting sun burnishing her skin. How she'd leaned in for the kiss that hadn't quite happened, how her tank top had clung to curves that shamed every bikini-filled billboard from here to Miami. Frustrated in more ways than one, he gave up on relaxing and shut off the tap.

As he toweled off, he caught the familiar ring of his cell phone. Crap, he'd forgotten. He always called his parents on Sunday evenings, just to touch base. It kept his mom happy and out of his hair, and let him and his dad do a bit of strategizing before the workweek started. Normally, he called around seven, and it was after nine.

Grabbing the phone, he perched on the edge of the bed, still dripping despite the towel around his waist.

"Hi, Mom…sorry I didn't call, I just got back to my room a little bit ago." He shifted farther onto the bed as they talked about his sisters, his grandmother and whether he had in fact gone to church. Suitably pacified, his mother turned him over to his father, who, like always, was ready to talk business. Nic half listened as his father reiterated the issues with the Vegas deal, issues they'd already discussed several times this week. But Lorenzo Caruso took the Boy Scout motto of "be prepared" seriously, and wanted to make sure they'd covered every contingency. Normally Nic was just as obsessive as his father, but tonight he just didn't have it in him.

"So what do you think of the Sandpiper property?" his father asked, grabbing his wandering attention.

Not the conversation Nic wanted to have right now. "It's got a good view, and most of the property is undeveloped. I'll know more after I meet with the people at City Hall tomorrow."

"We already knew all that, son. What I wanted to know were your impressions of the place. Is it good enough to be a Caruso property?"

"It's got potential," he hedged.

"Something wrong? Any problems down there I should know about?"

"Just some rumblings in town. It seems the Sandpiper is something of a local landmark. People aren't very happy about the idea of it being sold." One person in particular.

"They're just nervous about change. When they see the sketches for the resort, they'll love it. People always do. And the tourist money it brings in will shut down any complaints."

"Maybe."

"You okay, son?"

"Yeah, I'm fine. Just tired. It's been a long week-end." He explained about finding Murphy, helping Mrs. Rosenberg and touring the island. He left out any mention of his attraction to Jillian, or her feelings about the sale of the Sandpiper.

"So the dog's okay now, right?"

His father was a shark in the boardroom, but a big softie when it came to animals of any kind. "Yeah, he's healing up fine, according to Jillian."

"And this Jillian, she's a pretty girl?"

"What? Where did that come from?"

"You don't expect me to believe it was your mother's persuasive powers alone that got your butt in a church pew this morning, do you?" His father's chuckle carried over the line easily, despite the miles.

"Listen, it's not like that. Besides, have you ever tried telling Mom no?"

"Absolutely not, I'm no fool. But don't change the subject. This is the first time I've heard you talk about someone or something not related to work in longer than I can remember. I can only assume there's something special about her."

A mental picture of Jillian came unbidden. He rubbed a hand across his eyes and tried to sound disinterested. "She's pretty enough, and we had a good time. Nothing wrong with that."

"Agreed, nothing wrong with that at all. In fact, I'm happy to hear you had some downtime. Your mother and I worry about you. You work too hard."

"I do what needs to be done," he answered, hating how defensive he sounded.

"You do, and I'm grateful, and proud of your work ethic. But there's more to life than work."

"I do date, Dad. I'm not a monk." Although, come to think of it, he couldn't remember the last time he'd been out on a date. He'd given up on the idea of a real relationship years ago after the last in a string of girlfriends let it slip that she was more into his money than him. He wasn't willing to be anyone's sugar daddy.

For a while after that, he'd contented himself with casual flings. There had been a time when he'd been more than happy to pick up a girl in a hotel bar, but somehow he'd outgrown that lifestyle without really noticing. No wonder he was reacting to Jillian like she was a pool of water after a summer drought.

His dad laughed, triggering a wave of latent homesickness. Since when did he get homesick? "No one could accuse you of celibacy. But I didn't mean…dates. I'm talking about family, love, kids. The things that are really important in life, just as important as the job. I couldn't have gotten as far as I have without your mother by my side, you know that."

"Geez, Dad. I take it Mom's pining for grandkids again?"

"It's not just her, you know. I'd like to have a chance to get to see another generation of Carusos before I'm in the grave."

"You're not exactly elderly yet. But I'll make a note that providing the next generation of Carusos is another of my obligations to the family." He couldn't help the bitterness that crept into his voice. It was just never enough.

"Obligation? Hell, what's gotten into you? You think your mother's an obligation to me? Or you kids? Something I put on the schedule like a meeting with my broker?"

Now he'd stepped in it. He knew that his father adored his mother—he'd never seen a couple more in love. And they had raised their kids in that same love. Which was why he refused to settle for anything less now. "No, sir. I know that's not how it is."

"Damn straight. Love, family, those aren't obligations, they're blessings. The best part of life. I thought we'd raised you to know that. Your mother and I don't want you to miss out on that. We want the best for you, for all you kids."

Nic cleared his throat. "I'll keep that in mind." Good Lord, this was all too much right now.

"See that you do."

After exchanging goodbyes, Nic hung up the phone without getting out of the bed. Stretching out, still in nothing but his towel, he let his eyes drift closed. He'd get up and work on some reports in a few minutes.

But the exhaustion of the day had caught up with him, and he soon fell into a restless sleep, his dreams cluttered with barking dogs, bicycles and a blue-eyed siren he was forbidden to touch.

"Hey, Jillian, you there?"

Her head snapped up; she'd been daydreaming again. "Yes, sorry. Cassie, did you need me?"

"Just wanted to know if you were going to eat out back with Mollie and me. It's too nice to stay inside today." Cassie tossed her lab coat on her desk, and left by the rear clinic door, not waiting for an answer.

A break in the heat was rare this early in the year, and always welcome. Shaking off her lethargy, she closed up the chart she'd been working on and headed for the little seating area Cassie's father had built when he owned the clinic.

Stepping outside, she took a deep breath, relishing the lack of humidity for a change. By tomorrow the weather would probably be back to the normal sauna-like conditions, but today was pleasant and mild, with a taste of fall on the breeze. Cassie and Mollie were already sitting at the old-fashioned picnic table, a pitcher of iced tea between them as they ate their lunches.

Jillian set her own lunch on the table with the others, leftovers from the picnic she'd made for Nic yesterday. Remembering their uneasy arrangement had her stomach tumbling like a Tilt-A-Whirl. Unable to eat, she sipped some of the sweet tea instead, readying herself for the interrogation to come.

"So, spill it. How'd the date with Mr. Tall, Dark and Handsome go?" Mollie never was one to mince words. She called it like she saw it, usually an endearing trait. Not so much right now.

"Yeah, give us all the details so I can live vicariously through you," Cassie demanded, waggling a carrot stick at her.

"It wasn't a date. Just a...thank-you dinner."

"No hanky-panky?" Mollie asked.

"No!"

"Not even a good-night kiss?" Cassie prodded.

Jillian felt the heat rise in her cheeks.

"You're blushing!" Cassie clapped her hands in excitement. "You *did* kiss him! Was it amazing? God, I miss kissing."

"I am not blushing. I just got a lot of sun yesterday." As if they were going to buy that excuse. Her face was always a dead giveaway. "And yes, if you must know, we kissed. But it was just once…well, almost twice, but really just once."

That piqued both women's interest, the questions coming fast and furious.

"Whoa, slow down. There's nothing really to tell. We had lunch, he kissed me goodbye and then the next day, we did some biking and fishing."

"Two dates in two days, but there's nothing to tell? What happened?" Mollie's eyes crinkled in confusion. "I would have sworn I saw sparks flying when I ran into you at Pete's. Did he end up being a dud?"

Remembering the way she'd felt pressed against him, the way he'd made forgotten parts of her anatomy tingle, had her shaking her head. "No, not a dud. But things got…complicated."

"It's been a while since I've been with a man, but I don't remember it being that complicated. Slot A, Tab B, that kind of thing," Cassie countered.

"Cassie! Seriously? Get your mind out of the gutter. What I meant is, he isn't who I thought he was. He's not here on vacation, for one thing." At their blank looks, she added, "You know Caruso Hotels, right?"

"Of course," Cassie answered. "They've got that giant resort and casino down south, and I heard they're building one in Orlando, too. It's supposed to have its own water park and two nightclubs." She stopped, mouth dropping open. "Wait, Nic Caruso…he's one of *those* Carusos? What's he doing here?"

"He's here to see about buying the Sandpiper, that's what. They want to tear it down and use the land for one of their mega-resorts." The thought still stung. Sure, for him it was a job, not a personal attack, but the idea of her home being turned into some kind of twenty-four-hour tourist trap sure felt personal. At least being angry about it felt more useful than the tears did.

"What a lousy piece of—"

"Hold on, Mollie, it isn't settled yet. He says Caruso Hotels won't buy it if the grant goes through—they don't want the bad press of tearing down an historical site. And…he's going to help me with the grant application."

That bombshell had even Mollie speechless for once. Cassie regained her composure more quickly. "Wait, why would he help you if it would mess up his own plans?"

"Honestly, I'm not sure." She had lost hours of sleep trying to figure that one out. "He said he felt bad about not telling me who he was, but… I just don't know."

"I wouldn't trust him," was Mollie's response.

"Don't worry, I won't." Trust was earned as far as she was concerned; she'd learned that the hard way, growing up in foster care. Too many times she'd counted on someone, trusted them, only to have them leave without a backward glance. Better to rely only on yourself than to have your heart broken. She would never let someone shatter her that way again. No matter how tempting he was, she planned on keeping Mr. Nic Caruso a safe distance from her heart.

Chapter Eight

Jillian had overslept again today, after another night of tossing and turning. In fact, she hadn't slept well in weeks, not since she'd started working on the grant to save the Sandpiper. So much was riding on that application; she felt she had to get everything just right. If it wasn't for Nic's help, she would have gone crazy by now. She'd tracked down important events in the building's history using the library, but most of the technical work had been on his shoulders.

He had brought in an architect he knew to help them make sure they were describing all the building's attributes correctly, and then arranged for the land survey required. She just hoped it was enough. There was only so much grant money to go around, and as beautiful as the Sandpiper was, looks alone wouldn't cut it. Without any ties to important historical figures, the odds were long at best.

She'd mailed off the paperwork this morning, so now it was a waiting game.

That Nic was coming into town tonight hadn't helped her nerves, either. Having him call or chat on Skype every single night had been bad enough. The application didn't really require daily communication, but not a night had gone by that he hadn't spent time talking with her, asking her about her day, getting under her skin in a way that she hadn't expected.

Then he had offered to take her to dinner to celebrate the completion of the grant paperwork. She'd told herself it wasn't a date, not really. Just two friends marking the end of a business relationship. If she'd spent extra time choosing a dress to wear tonight, well, that was just because she didn't often get a chance to go somewhere as nice as Bayfront, where he'd made reservations. The sheer black dress had been a fun splurge, one both Cassie and Mollie had approved of when they had seen her hang it in the break room this morning. And the queasy feeling in her stomach was because she'd been too busy to eat lunch, nothing more.

At least after this it would be over. She'd gotten a bit too comfortable with their routine, snuggled into the couch, talking to him for hours every evening. That kind of closeness wasn't a good idea with someone like him, someone from a world so different from hers. She'd miss their chats, she could admit that, but that was all the more reason they needed to end. She'd have dinner with him tonight, but that would be their last contact until there was news of the grant, one way or the other.

Hoping to take her mind off the Sandpiper—and Nic—she grabbed the chart for the final patient of the day. She'd worked through lunch, and hoped this would be a quick case. She was eager for dinner, and still needed to change before Nic arrived. Before she entered the exam room to get the patient's vitals, she skimmed the notes Mollie had made.

Oh, God—no—this couldn't be right. The patient, Bailey, was a favorite at the clinic, a young beagle who'd never met a stranger. His owners, newlyweds in their late twenties, were just as friendly. Jillian always looked forward to their visits, which until now had consisted of routine checkups and the occasional ear infection. But, according to the notes in the chart, this was something altogether different.

It seemed that Bailey had been injured when jumping off the bed a few days ago, and at first he had been only mildly stiff. But instead of getting better, he'd gotten worse, and now was dragging both hind legs. Apprehensive, Jillian entered the room, hoping the young owner had exaggerated the symptoms. Maybe Bailey was just limping a bit, a little sore. One look, however, confirmed the worst. The normally exuberant pup was crouched in the corner, shaking instead of prancing for a treat, as was his normal habit. Elle Hancock, the beagle's mistress, was red-eyed from crying, and obviously struggling to hold it together.

Jillian felt like crying herself, but fought down her own emotions. She needed to project confidence for Bailey's sake, and Elle's. Gently lifting Bailey onto the table, she checked his temperature, pulse and respiration rate while Elle watched with concern.

"That's a good boy. You sure got yourself in trouble, didn't you, buddy? Don't you know better than to scare your mama like this? That's it, easy now." She finished her tasks and, reassuring Elle as much as she could, went to fetch Cassie. She found her in the lab, looking over an earlier patient's blood work results.

"Cassie?"

"One minute." She finished reading the report, then set it on the counter. "Who's next?"

"It's Bailey, and it's bad." She forced herself to be clinical. "I'm worried it's his back. You're going to need to take a look, but if we want to catch Dr. Rainer before he leaves for the day, I should have Mollie call as soon as possible." Dr. Rainer, the best veterinary neurologist in the state, was at least an hour's drive away. If they were going to transfer the paralyzed patient they'd need to start the process soon, or he wouldn't make it there before closing time.

"Oh, no, Bailey? Is he ambulatory?"

"Nope, totally down in the rear, not able to stand or walk at all."

"In that case, yeah, go ask Mollie to give Dr. Rainer a heads-up, then come join me in the exam room."

Cassie's very thorough exam was not encouraging. She tried to offer some hope, but cautioned that, with cases like this, there was a possibility the paralysis would be permanent—or worse—progress further. The prognosis wasn't good, and everyone in the room knew it.

With an increasing sense of dread, Jillian carried the patient beagle to the car. Elle followed with a copy of Bailey's medical records and driving directions to the specialist. As if sensing her unhappiness, Bailey squirmed, angling himself to lick her face in reassurance. The sweet creature was trying to comfort her, when he was the one so gravely injured. Touched, her tears spilled silently down her cheeks, soaking into the soft brown fur. Settling him on the seat of the car, she turned and hugged Elle, who had tear streaks of her own on her face. "Good luck. He's a strong, healthy dog, and Dr. Rainer's the best. You'll like her, I promise."

Elle simply nodded and got into the car. Jillian watched her drive away, then walked back inside, her legs almost too weak to carry her. Dazed and overwhelmed, she stood in the empty waiting room, unsure of what to do next. Intellectually, she knew that weeks of sleep deprivation and a skipped lunch were as much to blame for her reaction as concern for her patient, but the fear and grief were like a living thing, crushing her from the inside. On autopilot, tears still falling, she headed for the treatment room. There were patients that needed medications and lab equipment that needed to be taken care of before she could leave. She just had to get through the next half hour or so, then she would curl up somewhere and let the numbness swallow her.

For once traffic was cooperating, and Nic was fairly confident he could catch Jillian at the clinic before closing time. Maybe a smarter man would have stayed in Orlando after finishing his meetings, instead of heading for Paradise again. But being so close to Jillian without seeing her would take a stronger man than he had ever been or could ever hope to be. It was like he was addicted, and she was the drug. She'd slipped into his system somehow, and now he couldn't get her out. More surprisingly, he didn't want to get her out. Or let her go.

Of course, there was a chance that after seeing her in person, he'd find that she was just a woman like all the others, looking out for herself. Not the near-angel he'd come to think of her as during their nightly conversations. It had been her looks that caught his attention, but what had him reaching for the phone every night went deeper than that.

As they had worked on the complicated government forms, he'd found she had a sharp intellect tempered by an easy wit. Even more impressive was her determination. She had grit, and there was nothing he admired more. She certainly had to be tough to have made it through foster care, then living on her own and putting herself through school. He couldn't think of a more independent woman, and he'd certainly known his share, growing up with his mom and two sisters.

It was her independence, as much as anything, that made him feel comfortable getting as close as they had. He'd avoided entanglements for years, unable to handle being responsible for even one more person, as weighed down as he felt by work and family already. He hated that he sometimes resented the long hours and constant travel that he felt obligated to do. Even worse, he was starting to think of his family only in terms of the job, lumping them in with the rest of his to-do list.

Having one more person pushing him to be more, do more, might send him over the edge. And that's what women he dated always wanted: for him to work harder, make more money, gain more power for them to bask in. He didn't think Jillian was like that, but only time would tell. The more jaded part of him said that finding out wasn't worth the risk of being used again.

So why was he, even now, crossing over the Intracoastal, on his way to see a woman he had no business seeing? Because he couldn't do anything else, that's why. Being this out of control was a new feeling, one that didn't sit well. At least driving to Paradise Isle was taking action, and action was always better than inaction.

He'd see her, take her to dinner to celebrate the grant process being over, and maybe even get her out of his system for good.

Keeping that in mind, he pulled into the clinic parking lot just before six. He noted her tiny compact in the lot. Good, he hadn't missed her. Pleased that things were going according to plan, he locked his rental, the same style of SUV he'd rented before, and examined the building in front of him; he'd been in too big a hurry last time to notice many details. The low-slung building was in the same Spanish-style stucco as many of the other buildings on the street, with large glass windows lining the front, tinted against the brutal Florida sun. A nicely landscaped path took him to the front door, where he chuckled at a discreetly placed container of doggy pick-up bags. Swinging open the heavy door, he strode to the front desk, where Mollie and the doctor—Cassie something—had their heads together, whispering worriedly. He didn't see anyone else in the waiting area; from the state of the parking lot, he assumed the last clients must have already left.

"Hello, Mollie, Doctor. Is Jillian still here?" He'd seen her car, but it seemed presumptuous not to ask.

The two women looked at each other, as if conferring silently. The hair prickled on the back of his neck. Something wasn't right here. Something to do with Jillian. "What? What's going on? Where's Jillian?" Fear made his voice harsh, but damn it, how did they expect him to react?

The veterinarian spoke first, silencing Mollie with a gesture. "Jillian is in the back, finishing up with some overnight patients." She paused, as if she wasn't sure how to phrase what came next. "She...had a hard day.

She might not be up to dinner tonight. Maybe you could postpone?"

"Not possible. I'm only in town one night. I flew in this morning to finish up some details on our Orlando project, and I fly back out in the morning." What was going on here? "We've got reservations in an hour." He'd secured the seats at the elegant restaurant on a whim, one he was seriously rethinking. "Listen, if she doesn't want to go, or has other plans, just say so."

Mollie stood up, ignoring the other woman, and quickly made for the doorway to the next room. "I'll tell her you're here."

Nic turned back to the doctor. "You still haven't answered my questions, Doctor. So either you tell me what's going on, now, or I can force my way back there and see for myself. Either way, I'm not leaving until I know Jillian's okay. You choose." Someone was going to give him some answers, fast.

"Please, call me Cassie." The petite woman smiled, not in the least intimidated by his assertive demands. Oddly, that made him like her more, but he wasn't going to back down on his threat. "Jillian's a bit upset, that's all. One of her favorite patients just came in, critically injured. We've transferred him to a specialist, but his chances aren't good. It hit all of us hard, but Jillian particularly so. She's…not herself right now. I'm a bit worried about her being alone, so all in all, it's probably a good thing that you're here."

"Murphy?" He swallowed hard.

"Oh, no, not Murphy. Another patient, a sweet dog with really nice owners."

Hearing that the rascally border collie was safe had him relaxing the fists he hadn't known he'd been clenching. "But don't patients get hurt all the time? I mean, I get it, it's sad, but isn't that kind of business as usual?"

"Sure, and usually everyone handles it very professionally. You learn to keep your emotions in check, to be kind, but not get drawn into it. You have to. But sometimes…sometimes something happens and it's like all the pain is there at once, all that emotion you've managed to ignore over a hundred different patients swallows you up for a time. It happens to all of us, when we're tired, or stressed out, or just not up to par. A pint of rocky road and a good cry are the usual treatment, and then, when you finish crying, you're ready to do it all over again, see that next patient, face whatever the next challenge is." Her smile was weak, and couldn't hide the strain on her face.

He'd never really thought about how hard a job like this could be. It made his issues with zoning boards and contractors seem petty. That these women dealt with this kind of emotional trauma on a regular basis had him in awe. He'd be a basket case trying to deal with all that. So tonight he'd make sure to keep things light, cheer Jillian up, show her a good time. No problem.

Nic heard the treatment room door open behind him, and turned, a smile in place. Then he saw her, and his heart stuttered in his chest. Her face was tearstained, her normally pale skin blanched an unnatural white. He had to grip the counter in front of him to keep from picking her up and carrying her out of there.

Instead, he let her come to him. Gently, he placed a palm on her cheek, needing to touch her, but afraid she might shatter like a crystal if handled clumsily. She didn't so much as blink, just pressed her own palm against his hand, holding him to her. Her eyes, red from crying, pleaded with him, but for what? What could he do?

"She's been like this how long?" He kept his attention on Jillian, but his words, bitten past the lump in his throat, were for Cassie.

"About twenty, thirty minutes. She'll be okay. She just needs a little TLC."

"I just want to go home." Her words were clear, if quiet.

"I'm going to get you out of here, okay, honey?" He moved his hand down to her waist, steering her toward the front door. "Are you hungry?"

"She skipped lunch. We got swamped today, so I know she hasn't had anything since breakfast, if then," Cassie interjected, concern showing in the lines on her face.

"I…I didn't have breakfast, I overslept. But I'm not hungry right now. I'm fine, really."

Her voice sounded stronger, but he could see what the effort was costing her. She was ready to collapse, no two ways about it. No way was he letting her go home by herself. Cassie was right; she was in no condition to be alone right now.

Or to go to a fancy restaurant.

Fine. Problems cropped up in his work all the time; this was no different. He'd just come up with a new plan. Gears turning, he accepted the small purse and slinky black dress that Mollie retrieved for Jillian, then waved a brief goodbye as he escorted her out of the building.

When she stumbled, he held her tighter, half carrying her slender form by the time they reached his car. Using the button on the key fob to unlock it, he used his free hand to open the door, then simply lifted her up and into the seat. She was like deadweight in his arms, and her lack of protest scared him. She just sat there, eyes closed, so he reached over and buckled her in himself. Careful not to catch her hair in the door, he closed her in and ran around to the driver's side, starting the car with no real idea of where to go or what to do.

He headed for the Sandpiper. He'd reserved a room earlier, and they'd be able to get food there. Besides, it was as close to a home turf as he had right now.

Driving carefully, ridiculously afraid to jar her, he kept one eye on the road and one on her pale face. She appeared to be almost asleep, probably the best thing right now. His panic abating, he wanted to shake her for letting herself get so run-down. He'd known her to be resilient, practically invulnerable; seeing her this fragile made his heart ache in a way he didn't want to acknowledge. Instead, he focused on the task at hand, getting her to the inn, getting some food in her and then giving her hell for scaring him like this.

Plan in place, he pulled into the closest spot he could find in the Sandpiper parking lot. Rounding to her door, he touched her arm, again struck by how cold she felt. Her eyes opened at his touch. "Hey, honey, we're here. Can you get out?"

She nodded, taking in their surroundings without a word. If she was surprised he'd brought her to the inn instead of her apartment, she didn't show it. She could question his motives later. Right now, he just wanted to get her to his room safely. After that? He didn't have a clue.

Chapter Nine

Jillian wandered the lobby of the inn while Nic checked in with the front desk. It had been a while since she'd seen the inside, but not much had changed. The natural orchids in the coquina fireplace caught her eye; it must be too early in the year for a fire. Too bad, she would appreciate the warmth right now. She was cold down to her bones. Served her right for skimping on meals and sleep. Nic must think she was an idiot, acting like some kind of trauma victim over an injured dog. She would have tried to explain in the car, but she was just too tired. Just thinking about putting that many words together was exhausting. She desperately wanted to flop down in one of the lobby chairs, but if she sat down, she might not get back up again.

Finished at the desk, Nic motioned for her to follow. Maybe he wanted to drop his stuff off before taking her back to her place? Why else would he have brought her here? Or did he bring her here so she could change into her dress? Did he still want to go out to dinner? Nothing made sense to her frazzled brain, and trying to figure it out made her head hurt. Better to go along with whatever he was planning, and figure it all out later.

He led her up a flight of stairs, catching her elbow when she almost missed a step. At the landing he went right and opened the last door off the hallway. Watching her, he paused, then gestured for her to go in.

Of course, ladies first. Always the gentleman. An absurd giggle threatened to bubble up, another sure sign she was way over her emotional limit for the day.

Inside, he locked the door, set her purse on the nightstand and strode directly to the bathroom. Left to wait again, she checked out the room. She'd never been in one of the Sandpiper's guest rooms, and this one was certainly worth seeing. A king-size sleigh bed dominated the room, its carved cherry headboard an art piece in itself. A small sitting area with two wingback chairs sat in front of the balcony doors, and a low dresser with a flat-screen television on top completed the furniture. Turning to take it all in, she found Nic standing at the bathroom door, watching her.

"I ran you a bath, put whatever bubble stuff they had in it. It should warm you up. I'll order the food while you're taking your bath." His words were clear, but she couldn't wrap her head around his meaning.

"You want me to take a bath?"

"You're cold, and you're upset. My sisters swear by long baths when they're upset. My mom, too. I thought it might help."

"I don't know…"

"Just take the bath. Then we can talk, or not talk, what-ever." He scrubbed a hand over his face. "Listen, I'm not trying to seduce you or anything, okay? Just take the bath, please?"

It was the "please" that got to her. She knew adding it on had cost him. And really, a bath did sound wonder-ful. Her apartment only had a glassed-in shower stall, no tub. Stretching out in the big claw-foot one behind him would be heavenly. And warm, so very warm. Giving in, she nodded. "Okay."

He stepped aside so she could pass, saying nothing, but looking relieved when she went into the bathroom and shut the door. Stripping quickly, ignoring her ap-pearance in the mirror, she sank into the fragrant bub-bles. The scent of lavender and honeysuckle rose up on the steam, making her feel like she was floating on flower petals instead of water. Heat seeped into her, re-leasing the muscles she had been clenching in a desper-ate attempt to keep from falling apart. Letting herself slide down the tub, she submerged to her ears, and tuned the world out for a few blessed minutes.

Cocooned in the fragrant water, her thoughts turned to the man that had brought her here. Who would have thought a straitlaced corporate executive would have such a sensitive side? She would have bet money he was going to bail when he saw her falling apart like that—she'd seen the fear and confusion in his eyes—but instead he'd rushed to her side, supported her, been there for her.

Nothing in her background had prepared her for that kind of reaction. No one had ever really been there for her, taken care of her. The Marshalls, Cassie's family, had tried, but she'd been too distrustful to let them get close. So they'd mostly let her take care of herself, which was exactly what she'd wanted and needed. Foster care and living on her own so young had taught her to be independent, no matter what.

As much as she said she wanted a husband and a family someday, the idea of actually letting down her guard, being that close, that dependent on anyone, had always terrified her. But with Nic it felt natural. Easy. Safe. Who knew that giving up a bit of control could feel so right?

Creak...

She sat bolt upright at the sudden sound, only to immediately slosh back under the bubbles when she saw Nic at the door. "What are you doing in here? Get out!"

"I knocked, but you didn't answer. I was afraid you'd fallen asleep in there." He had one hand over his eyes; the other was clutching a stack of clothing. "I brought you some sweatpants and a T-shirt. I thought you might want to change when you were done, and that dress didn't look very comfortable."

She wouldn't have heard his knock with her ears submerged. But still! "Just leave them there and get *out*." Mortified, she slid farther under the water, hoping everything was covered. She didn't trust him not to peek between his fingers. Just the thought of him seeing her nude warmed her blood, despite the rapidly cooling water. Nic Caruso definitely heated things up, that's for sure.

When she was sure he was gone, she jumped out of the tub, then darted to the door to lock herself in. Heart pounding, she grabbed a towel and dried herself hurriedly, feeling exposed despite the locked door between them. She threw on the too-big clothes, the soft shirt falling nearly to her knees. The pants she cinched with the drawstring, and then rolled up the legs so she wouldn't trip.

Fully covered, she stopped to catch her breath and mop up the water she'd sloshed onto the floor in her mad dash to lock the door. She ignored the fogged-up mirror; a quick finger comb of her curls was the best she could do appearance-wise, anyway. Her makeup was in her purse in the other room. Not that she was trying to impress him. They both knew that anything between them was completely impossible. No point in getting worked up over what was, in the end, just a business relationship.

After closing the door, Nic sank down onto the edge of the bed. He really had been concerned she might have fallen asleep in there. But his brotherly compassion had flown the coop when she'd jolted into a sitting position, suds streaking down her slick skin. He'd covered his eyes as quickly as he could, but not before he'd seen more than he should, more than was good for him. The image of all that creamy skin, slick and rosy from the bathwater, was going to be branded in his brain forever.

Adjusting his suddenly too-tight pants, he debated calling down to room service again to ask for some whiskey, something to take the edge off. On the other hand, if he was going to have any hope of taking care of her needs, rather than focusing on his own less honorable ones, he needed to stay sober. Otherwise, he was liable to forget what a bad idea being together was, and in her weakened condition that would be unforgivable. He might be a hot-blooded guy, but he knew not to take advantage of a woman; his father had drilled that lesson into him by the time he hit puberty. Which meant he needed to keep his libido locked down, even if it killed him.

The click of the bathroom door signaled her return. She edged out around the door, and he knew he was doomed. Seeing her in his shirt, his clothes, was like a sucker punch to the gut. The soft material clung to her curves, her hair was damp and curling around her face, and her big eyes were even darker against her still-too-pale skin. She was softness, and vulnerability, and everything he thought he didn't want, didn't need, all bundled up in a package hot enough to melt steel. Absently, he pressed a hand against the aching in his chest. Dear God, what was he going to do with her?

Worse, what was she doing to him?

"I'm sorry."

Her voice jump-started his stalled mental capacities. "What?" Yeah, that sounded brilliant.

"I said I'm sorry. I don't know what got into me. I'm never like that." She fiddled with the drawstring to his too-big sweatpants. The innocent movement had his hormones swirling again. The lady was killing him slowly and she had no idea she was doing it.

"Like what?"

"Weak." Her eyes dropped at the word.

Crossing to her, he lifted her chin, his fingers burning where they met her skin. "Not weak. Human. We all have a breaking point, honey. Today, you hit yours."

She offered a shy smile, then broke contact by stepping past him, toward the sitting area. "I shouldn't have skipped lunch, it was stupid. We were just so busy and—"

"And you were taking care of everyone else but yourself. Am I right?" He cocked an eyebrow, daring her to contradict him.

She raised her chin, defensiveness radiating off her.

"That's my job. It's not like I was doing my nails or something. I was busy."

Good, she was getting her spunk back. "I get that. I get busy, too. But you've got people and their pets depending on you, so try for some balance, okay? Stock some snacks in the break room for when you're busy, or protein shakes, whatever. Being busy doesn't have to mean letting your blood sugar crash. You're smarter than that." He really did hope she would listen; she'd scared the crap out of him. If pushing her buttons would get her to take better care of herself, he was more than willing to do it.

Looking chastened, she shrugged. "You're right. It was dumb."

"Like I said, we all have bad days."

"I bet you've never cried on the job."

The image of him crying in the middle of some business deal had the corners of his mouth twitching. "No, I guess not. But I do yell, and I bet you don't do that."

"No, I guess I don't," she conceded. Her stomach rumbled audibly. "I'm too hungry to keep arguing. I think I could eat a horse."

"Well, horse wasn't on the menu, but hopefully burgers and fries will work. I'd planned to take you out for steak and champagne, but comfort food and a movie on pay-per-view seemed like a better idea, given the circumstances."

"A burger sounds heavenly right now. Then we'll see about a movie."

A knock at the door signaled the arrival of room service. Nic opened the door for a teenager pushing a wheeled cart with an assortment of covered dishes. The food was transferred to the sitting table, along with two sodas, napkins and tableware. Nic signed the receipt, gave a generous tip and closed the door. Turning back to the table, he let Jillian choose her chair, then settled in the one opposite. "I hope soda is okay. I thought it might help get your blood sugar up quickly, in case you weren't ready for a meal yet."

"It's fine, and I'm more than ready to eat, trust me."

Trust. She threw the word out casually, but they both knew it wasn't as easy as all that. Trust had to be earned, and even then you could still get burned. He trusted his family, sure, but he'd seen too many handshake deals gone wrong, seen too many wealthy men used by women as nothing more than a meal ticket, to be willing to accept anything or anyone at face value. That Jillian, sitting there, barefaced, in his old clothes, could make him want to let down his hard-won barriers was absolutely terrifying. He'd been worried about not hurting her, but now he realized she held the power to hurt him, as well. And that was something he could not allow.

Jillian attacked her burger with a vengeance. She felt like her stomach was turning itself inside out, she was so hungry. Her embarrassing outburst had sapped her remaining reserves, leaving her hollowed out in more ways than one. The juicy burger would fill some of that emptiness, but not all of it. Work, her friendship with Cassie and Mollie, her church, the animals, they helped, but at the end of the day there was still a dark hole deep down inside. One she hadn't been aware of until she met Nic.

Rolling her eyes at her own melodrama, she concentrated on the good food in front of her instead of the man across the table. He must think she was some kind of basket case. No need to make it worse by mooning over him. Only when the last fry was gone, and as much of the burger as she could stuff in, did she risk conversation.

"So I never did ask why you had to come back to Orlando. I thought you were working over in, where was it—South Carolina—this week?"

"I was able to wrap up that deal yesterday, but there were some environmental issues to address at the Orlando site, so I flew in this morning. I met with the landscape architect and the environmental group, got them to come up with a compromise that provided the drainage we need while protecting the native species in the area. And of course, I wanted the chance to celebrate with you."

"I'm sorry we missed our reservations." Her burger suddenly felt heavy in her stomach. He'd had such a long day, then driven all the way out here to treat her to dinner, and instead of a celebration he'd ended up playing nursemaid.

"Hey, I told you, you have nothing to be sorry for." His deep voice brooked no argument. "Besides, I'd rather eat burgers in a T-shirt than lobster in a suit any day."

He did look content, and all male, leaning back in that big chair, long legs sprawled out in front of him. His T-shirt—he must have changed while she was in the tub—stretched across his broad shoulders and well-defined chest, making him look more like a male model than a businessman. But the casual clothes did nothing to detract from the energy that radiated off him. Men like him didn't need power suits to be intimidating; they were just born that way.

Watching him, mesmerized by all that maleness, she didn't even notice the buzzing coming from her purse.

"Is that your phone?"

"My phone? Oh, crud, yes, my phone! I forgot to turn it off vibrate when I left work." She dove onto the bed to grab her purse, retrieving her phone before the voice mail could kick in. Spotting Cassie's number on the caller ID had her burger threatening to come back up. *Please, please, don't be bad news.*

"Hey Cassie, do you have news on Bailey?" She listened to Cassie's report, tears stinging her eyes, heart in her throat. "Are they sure? Oh, thank God! Does Elle know? Wonderful! Okay, let me know if there's anything I can do." She gave Nic a quick thumbs-up when he sank down on the bed beside her. "All right, see you Monday. And thanks again for calling."

She hung up and turned, the tiredness gone, her smile stretching so wide she thought her face might break in half.

"Good news, I take it?"

"The best. His test results looked better than expected, and he's already responding to the intravenous medication they're giving him. It will take a while, but they think he'll make a full recovery. He's going to be okay!"

Overwhelmed, she threw her arms around him, hugging him in celebration. Her face pressed to his shoulder, she inhaled his clean, spicy scent as he returned the embrace. He felt strong and safe, his muscles hard beneath her hands. Then his arms tightened around her, and that quickly the moment shifted. Her breathing quickened as one of his hands began to rub sensuous circles up and down her back. Melting, she yielded to the pressure, arching into him, her head bowed back to the kiss she craved as much as her next breath.

He met her halfway. His mouth came down over hers, tasting and then plundering as he lifted her into his lap.

Her hands roamed his body, testing the muscles beneath. His fingers wrapped in her hair, pinning her in place as their tongues danced to a silent rhythm.

Head spinning, she clung to him, fists bunching in his shirt as heat pulsed beneath her skin. Every cell in her body was screaming that this was right, he was right. Deep inside, something clicked, as if the tumblers of a lock were falling in place.

Greedy, hungry for more, she pressed even closer, swept up in the magic he wove with his hands and lips, knowing now that she needed him, more than she'd ever needed anyone.

Holding Jillian was like holding a live wire, her soft curves lighting up his body wherever she pressed against him. Her hands electrified nerve endings everywhere she touched, daring his body to respond. Nuzzling his way from her lips to her slender neck, he tumbled them both to the bed, angling her so her compact body landed on top of his own hardness.

"Ouch!"

A sharp pain shot through his back, just below his rib cage. "What the…" Moving Jillian to the side, he rolled and reached for the unseen weapon. "A fork?"

"What? Oh, no, I must have dropped it when I was grabbing for the phone. I was so worried it would be bad news, I forgot it was in my hand." Giggling, she bit her bottom lip. "Are you okay?"

She was laughing? The most intense kiss in his life ends with him being stabbed in the back, and she was laughing at him? Lobbing a pillow at her head, he grunted out, "It's not funny. I could have been seriously injured."

"Uh-huh."

"This is serious." He tried to sound stern, but knew he'd failed. The truth was, it was serious, way too serious, given that he was leaving first thing in the morning. They'd come very close to crossing a line, one he had promised himself he wouldn't cross, not while she was weak and vulnerable.

As if trying to diffuse the situation, Jillian scooted up to the top of the bed, carefully keeping to her side, and grabbed the remote. Eyes averted, she focused on the flat-screen television across from the bed. "You promised me a movie, didn't you?"

Willing to play along, knowing this wasn't the time to push things, he stretched himself out next to her, plumping a pillow under his head. "Yes, ma'am. Lady's choice."

Less than an hour into the movie, Jillian's slow, even breathing told him she had fallen asleep. Should he wake her up, take her home? She didn't have to work tomorrow; he knew it was her one weekend off this month. It seemed a shame to disturb her when she was so tired. If she stayed, it would be torture to lie beside her all night, without touching, but the idea of waking up beside her was oddly tempting.

Ignoring the warning bells in his head, he kissed her forehead and pulled the covers over her, settling himself in for a long night. Despite the lingering sexual tension, listening to her breathing proved more relaxing than he would have predicted. He was on the verge of drifting off himself when he heard her cell phone ringing.

Please, not more bad news, not now. Teeth clenched,

he grabbed the phone from the table and answered it himself, as she slowly stirred beside him.

"Hello?"

"Who's this? Where's Jillian?" The voice sounded oddly familiar.

"This is Nic. Jillian's right here. Can I tell her who's calling?" Jillian was sitting up now, reaching for the phone, rubbing her eyes.

"It's Vivian Rosenberg, that's who! Now let me talk to Jillian!" Handing the phone to Jillian he made the connection. Rosenberg? As in Murphy's owner? Had something happened to the dog? Listening to Jillian's reassurances that she'd be right there, wherever *there* was, he quickly found and put on socks and shoes, handing Jillian hers, as well. Keys in hand, he was ready to go when she hung up.

"Murphy got away again. Mrs. Rosenberg had the senior group over tonight for cards, and in the confusion of everyone leaving, he slipped out." She slipped on her shoes, then grabbed the plastic bag he'd given her to put her clothes in after her bath.

"We'll find him," he assured her, already unlocking the door.

"We? Oh, Nic, you don't have to come. You can just drop me off at the clinic. I've got my car there."

"No way. I'm going with you. It's late, and however safe Paradise is, you shouldn't be running around in the dark by yourself."

She rolled her eyes, but didn't protest. "Fine, let's just hurry."

They made for the car and were on the road within minutes, both of them scouring the streets for signs of Murphy on the way to Mrs. Rosenberg's. As they entered her neighborhood, he remembered something he'd been wondering about. "Why did she call you, not the clinic, or animal services or something?"

"Well, I've been going over there every day to take Murphy for a run, do some training with him. She knows I love him just as much as she does, that I'd want to be the one to look for him. Plus, he knows me, so he's more likely to come if he hears me calling."

"You go over there every day?"

"Well, not tonight, obviously. But yeah, either before or after work, ever since his last escape attempt. She still wants me to keep him, but since I can't, this is the best I can do, and the exercise keeps him out of trouble. Usually." She smiled, but it didn't reach her eyes. "It's almost like having my own dog."

They rode in silence the rest of the way, him wondering at the bond she'd forged with Murphy, and the dedication it took to go take care of yet another animal after a full day of doing just that at the clinic. Every time he thought he knew her, she impressed him again. That someone so dedicated to pets couldn't have one of her own struck him as incredibly sad, but she had made the best of it, like she did with everything. Hopefully, she'd be able to do the same if Caruso Hotels bought the Sandpiper.

Sobered by the thought, he let Jillian take the lead when they reached Mrs. Rosenberg's. The elderly woman handed out flashlights, clutching a fuchsia robe around her, seemingly unconcerned that Nic was with Jillian at this late hour. He'd wondered if she'd say something, and was glad when she didn't. He didn't want Jillian having to deal with small-town gossip about their relationship. Especially since he hadn't figured out how they could ever have a relationship. He had a job to do, and he couldn't ignore it for the sake of one woman, no matter how bewitching she was. Which meant he'd keep the Caruso legacy moving forward, and hope it didn't push her out of his life entirely.

Chapter Ten

Flashlight in hand, Jillian tried to figure out where to start looking. Her head was such a tangle right now, she wasn't sure she could find her way out of a paper bag, much less locate a stubborn pup with a nose for trouble. "I always use the same route when I take him on his run, and dogs can be creatures of habit. Maybe he was frustrated because I didn't come today, and followed it on his own."

"Makes as much sense as anything. Lead the way." Nic held a flashlight, a bottle of water and Murphy's leash. Jillian had dog treats and the other flashlight. Together they started down the quiet suburban street, taking turns calling for the dog. At each clump of trees, she'd stop and check the shadows before moving on to the next bush, the next yard, the next block.

The moon was bright above the horizon, creating a

silver-tinged landscape that would have been romantic under any other circumstances. Jasmine blew on the breeze, sweetening the evening, despite the fear that gripped her. Poor Murphy. His training was progressing, but with the limited time she had to spend with him, he still wasn't trustworthy around doors. And Mrs. Rosenberg, bless her heart, wasn't up to the challenge he presented. If he was hers full-time, she could have had him well under control by now, but her landlord wasn't budging. Just one more dream that wasn't going to come true.

Watching Nic as he checked yet another hedge, she sighed. He was another dream that wasn't going to be realized. The past few weeks, she'd gotten to see the man behind the business suit, and she liked what she saw. His workaholic nature was driven not by blind ambition, but by a desire to do right by his family. She knew he looked up to his father, that he was determined to live up to the trust placed in him. That kind of family loyalty was rare, and she couldn't help but respect him for it. Even though that same family loyalty could mean the destruction of her little island sanctuary.

"Do you think he would have gone this far?" Nic asked as they crossed yet another deserted street.

"I honestly don't know. He's fast, so he could have covered a lot of ground pretty quickly if he wanted to. On the other hand, if he was sniffing every fence post and fire hydrant, it could take him all week just to circle the block." She huffed to blow her hair out of her face. She hadn't thought to grab a hair tie when they ran out of the hotel. "If it was daytime, we could ask if anyone had seen him, but as it is…" Her voice trailed off.

"Yeah, this place really does roll up the streets after dark, doesn't it?"

They hadn't seen anyone since they'd started their walk. Most of the houses were quiet, the warm glow of porch lights acting as sentries against the night. "I guess Paradise is pretty boring after Vegas and New York City, huh?" She kicked at some mulch that had spilled over onto the sidewalk from its assigned flower bed. This might be her idea of perfection, but to him it was just some Podunk town. No wonder he was so eager to bring in tourists and nightclubs, to make it another Daytona or South Beach.

"Boring? No, that's not how I would describe it. Peaceful was more what I was thinking. It's actually kind of nice to be somewhere where everyone goes home at night, has dinner with the family and turns out the lights. I'd forgotten people still lived like this."

His wistful tone took her by surprise. Had she been wrong to assume he couldn't see what she saw? "Before I moved here, I didn't know people could live this way. I love seeing kids playing in the yards every evening, old men hanging out at the hardware store in the morning. Life on the mainland is always changing, but here on the island, they've managed to hold on to what's important. That predictability makes me feel…safe, I guess."

The rhythms of Paradise Isle were like a security blanket she tucked around herself to help her sleep at night. After so many moves, changes and families, she had finally found a place where she felt secure. That he could tear that all apart was the elephant in the room, a fact both of them were unwilling to confront.

"The town I grew up in was like this, but I guess I

thought that because I had changed, everyone else, every-where else, had changed, too." He looked directly at her, as if holding her with his gaze. "I'm glad I was wrong."

Before she could decide exactly what he meant by that, a faint sound had her attention shifting. "Did you hear that?"

"What?"

She heard it again…a high-pitched whine, almost a whimper. "That!"

"Maybe…yeah, I hear it. Think that's Murphy?"

"I don't know, but it doesn't sound good." Pacing, she tried to locate where the sound was coming from. Maybe it was a bit louder, a bit stronger in that direction. Maybe.

Frustrated, she walked more quickly. "Murphy! Is that you, boy?" An answering bark and more whining had her running, Nic's footsteps heavy behind her. The distressed sounds grew louder, coming from behind the last house on the block.

Ignoring Nic's protest, she darted right into the yard and around the side of the house. At this point, she could hear two animals; the whining one was, hopefully, Murphy. But what was that hissing, growling noise? A possum? They could really do some damage; a raccoon would be even worse. Heart in her throat, she scanned the small backyard, hoping the poor dog wouldn't be too injured.

There, in the corner, she could make out Murphy's white patches in the moonlight. Approaching cautiously, Nic at her side, she brandished the flashlight like a weapon, hoping desperately she wouldn't have to use it.

Nic grabbed Jillian's arm, slowing her before she could barrel headfirst into whatever had Murphy cowering in the shadows by the fence. Didn't she understand how dangerous this was? They were in a stranger's yard late at night, chasing what might be some kind of rabid beast. And she was ready to jump in without thought to her own safety, an idea as foolhardy as it was admirable. "Let me go first, see what we're dealing with."

"No way. I'm the one with the animal background, and I'm more familiar with the wildlife around here," she snapped, trying to pull away from him.

His instinct was to argue, but before he could come up with something that sounded like more than macho rhetoric, the clouds parted, letting moonlight flood the yard. There, only a few feet away, standing guard on top of a large trash can, was Murphy's would-be attacker.

"Oh, Murphy..." Jillian's reproach dissolved into a full-fledged laugh.

A cat. The creature they'd heard hissing and screeching was nothing more than a big old tomcat, defending his territory from the hapless canine.

Shaking his head, Nic ignored the angry sentry and went to the trembling dog. "Big tough dog like you, afraid of a little pussycat? You should be ashamed of yourself." He gave the dog a good-natured pat and reached for the bag of treats Jillian had brought. "Here you go, liver treats. Maybe they'll give you some courage." The cat, assured of its victory, stretched and then proceeded to carefully groom itself. Still, Nic gave it a wide birth, if only to spare Murphy any further trauma.

"We'd better get out of here before whoever lives here comes out to investigate," Jillian warned, her eyes darting to a light that now glowed in an upstairs window.

"Good idea." Explaining this ridiculous rescue mission to a half-asleep homeowner didn't sound like fun. And they really needed to get Murphy back to Mrs. Rosenberg before the poor lady made herself sick with worry. "Let's move."

They'd made it a full block before his pulse settled down, and he was able to appreciate the humor in the situation. Murphy was back to his normal carefree self by then, as well, and he danced at the end of the leash, eager to be home.

As he walked with the happy dog down the quiet street, Jillian by his side, he was struck by the normalcy of it all. The longing behind that thought surprised him. Sure, he'd become disillusioned with the constant travel of his current lifestyle, but did that mean he wanted something so completely different? Lately, he had toyed with the idea of shifting some travel responsibilities to other people in his department, spending more time at his office in the city. But would that be enough? He had thought it would be. But then why did he feel more at home, more at peace, here on this tiny island, than he ever had in New York City?

Shoving away the questions that circled him like hungry sharks, he chose to focus on the here and now. Right now he was strolling under a starry sky with a beautiful, intelligent, courageous woman. Reaching out, he caught her hand in his, letting them swing together as they walked. She accepted the gesture without hesitation, perhaps trapped by the same magic that had him wishing for things that weren't his to wish for. If there was a way to freeze this moment, keep it and take it out whenever he wanted, he would.

They reached the street that Mrs. Rosenberg lived on

far too soon, his steps slowing as they approached the house. When they reached the walkway, Jillian slipped her hand away, a shy smile on her face. The spell that had entangled them was unraveling, taking a part of him with it.

"Is that you, Jillian? Did you find him? Is he okay?" Mrs. Rosenberg called from her front porch, peering out into the night.

"Yes, Mrs. Rosenberg, we have him. He's fine, other than some bruising to his ego. He got cornered by a cat over on Hibiscus Street."

The elderly woman waved them over, eager to be reunited with the dog that gave her so much trouble. "You poor thing, was that cat mean to you? Mama will make it up to you, don't you worry." Murphy accepted her praise and subsequent petting with a big doggy grin, tongue hanging out one side of his mouth. "You two, do you want to come in and have a drink or a snack? I've got plenty of cookies left from our little card party."

Jillian responded first. "No, but thank you. It's been a long day, and I really need to go home and get some sleep."

The older woman scrutinized the younger and then nodded, apparently accepting her excuse as valid. "You do that then, and sleep in tomorrow, too, if you can. Murphy can wait for his run until later. I'll keep him locked down until then."

"Sounds good," Jillian replied.

"And you, young man. Don't think I'm not wondering why you were with my Jillian at this hour. I'm just too well-mannered to say anything about it. But I'm watching you, and you'd better have the right kind of intentions, if you know what I mean."

The right kind of intentions? Who said things like that? He might have laughed if she didn't look so very serious. Not wanting to hurt her feelings or dig himself any deeper, he decided to play it safe. "Yes, ma'am. I understand." Which was a bold-faced lie. Right now, he didn't understand anything, least of all his intentions toward Jillian.

Jillian settled into the comfortable bucket seat as Nic drove her home. She was exhausted, too many near ca-tastrophes in too short a time, but the energy crackling between them kept her alert. The passionate embrace at the inn had ignited more sparks between them, and the walk with Murphy had layered a new element of sweet-ness onto the sultry feelings he inspired.

Chemistry was crazy that way. She'd been on numer-ous dates with totally suitable men, men from her own neighborhood with similar lifestyles and goals, and felt nothing more than curiosity. But Nic, who was all wrong for her, and completely unattainable, made her pulse throb and her knees weak every time he came near. To-tally unfair, and at the moment, incredibly disturbing.

Would he expect a kiss when he dropped her off? Or more—would he want to pick up where they'd left off before an errant piece of silverware had so pointedly interrupted them?

Of course, the most likely scenario was that he was berating himself for that lack of judgment and trying to figure out how to let her down easy. After all, this was just one stop in his busy schedule. For all she knew, he had dinner, and maybe more, with women at every job site. Not to mention that currently she and the Island Preservation Society were a huge thorn in his side with regards to his business dealings. And with Nic, nothing was ever just business; it was always personal, always about how best to impress his family. Which meant if the grant fell through, his connection to her wouldn't be enough to stop him from buying, and destroying, the Sandpiper. For him, it was a matter of family loyalty, something she would never begrudge him, no matter how it affected her personally.

Hoping to avoid an awkward scene, or the lack of one for that matter, she had a hand on the door handle, ready to jump out the minute he pulled up to the clinic. "Thanks for the ride, and dinner, and helping with Murphy and, well, everything," she fumbled, nerves getting the best of her. "I'll, um, talk to you later."

Nic, with his quick reflexes, bounded out of the car and was at her side before she finished extricating herself from the SUV. He reached into the backseat, retrieving her purse and dress, both of which she'd nearly forgotten in her cowardly bid at a quick getaway. He ignored her attempt to take them from him, instead carrying them to her car, where he took the time to put them on the passenger's seat before opening the driver's door for her. His automatic chivalry gave her weary heart yet another jolt. His touch, a soft brush of his knuckles against her cheek, nearly broke her.

Their eyes locked, heat and longing and something more spilling into the stillness between them. She watched, helpless to stop him, not wanting to stop him, as Nic leaned into her, then closed her eyes against the sudden, sharp sting of tears when he only placed a gentle, chaste kiss on her forehead.

"We need to talk about us, Jillian. Not tonight, but soon. I'm not done here." His voice was husky; hers had abandoned her entirely. A simple nod was the best she could manage before retreating into the relative safety of her car. She somehow shut and locked the door in a single motion. Locking him out, or herself in?

Chapter Eleven

It had been a full week since Murphy's last escape and everything that had happened that night. She'd spent much of that time dodging Nic's phone calls. Now that the work on the grant proposal was over, there was no reason for him to contact her, but he still called every night, like clockwork. What had he meant when he said he wasn't done? What more was there?

It was not like they'd been dating, or even friends really. They'd had a moment of passion, some tender moments. They both knew that wasn't enough to build a relationship on. So any lingering emotion was misplaced and should be ruthlessly ignored. To that end, she'd agreed to meet Mollie for an afternoon at the beach; a few hours of sun and sand could fix pretty much anything. And just in case, she'd picked up Murphy on her way over. Now that his paws were healed, he was in need of some playtime, and his high spirits were guaranteed to chase any blues away.

She held the leash tight and let Murphy sniff each weather-beaten stair step on the way down to the sand. His nose quivered with delight at all the new smells, and his black-and-white plume of a tail wagged high over his back. His enthusiasm was impossible to resist. Happier already, she kicked her flip-flops off and left them at the base of the stairs before breaking into a jog over the hot sand, heading for the cooler, hard-packed sand closer to the water. Murphy barked with delight, happy to chase the pipers and gulls that skittered along the shoreline.

At Murphy's bark, Mollie, comfortably situated in a low-slung beach chair right at the water's edge, looked up from her book and smiled. "I didn't know you were bringing this handsome guy. Has he been behaving himself lately?"

"More or less, depending on the day. But no more escape attempts. I figure a few hours at the beach should wear him out enough to keep him home for a while." She passed the leash to Mollie so she could put down the chair she'd been carrying, unfolding it and situating it next to Mollie's. From her bag she withdrew a rubber ball. Murphy spotted it and immediately crouched down in the famous border collie stance, ready to leap the minute it was tossed. Unsnapping the leash, she threw the toy into the waves before settling into her chair.

"So has he called yet?" Mollie asked.

"Who?" Jillian feigned ignorance.

Mollie wasn't fooled. "You know who. Mr. Caruso Hotels himself. Have you heard from him?"

"Yes. I mean, no." At Mollie's raised eyebrow, she continued, "He's called. A lot. I just don't answer. He'd promised to help with the grant, and he did, but that's over now. There's no reason for us to talk now."

"No reason at all, except the guy is crazy about you."

She dropped the dripping ball she'd been about to throw, her fingers unresponsive. "What? You're crazy. It was just business."

Mollie lifted her sunglasses to scrutinize her friend. "Are you telling me nothing happened between you?"

Jillian looked down to watch the water creeping closer to her chair. "There's some…chemistry. I won't deny that. But he's probably got women throwing themselves at him all the time. A girl in every port, you know." Just saying the words hurt, but she might as well face the truth.

"I don't buy it. If just any girl would do, he wouldn't have driven all the way from Orlando to take you to dinner." The petite brunette shook her head, her short hair swinging. "No, that wasn't some booty call. The man cares about you. Otherwise, he would have ditched you the other night when he saw what a basket case you were."

"I was not a basket case."

"Sweetie, you were in rough shape. Most men would have run fast and far from that kind of drama. Instead, he went all protective alpha male—I swear I thought he was going to pick you up and carry you off. I may have even swooned a little."

The image of tomboy Mollie swooning made Jillian smile. "He *was* awfully sweet," she conceded. "But the fact is, there's nothing going on between us, and no reason to keep in contact. At least not until we find out about the grant."

Mollie frowned. "What do you think the chances are of saving the Sandpiper?"

"Not great." She sighed, absently rubbing Murphy's ears. "We applied late in the year, so there won't be much money left, even if they like the proposal. And although the Sandpiper is certainly old enough and still reflects the original architecture, most of the buildings that are selected have some kind of tie-in to Florida history or to a famous person. The Sandpiper is meaningful to us, but that isn't enough to impress the committee."

"If it doesn't go through, will Nic really buy it and tear it down? Even though he knows how much it will upset you?

"It's not really his call. Caruso Hotels is a giant corporation. He's just doing his job." Why was she defending him?

"But he has to have a say in it. He's a vice president, isn't he? Can't you get him to back off?"

"What, ask him to set aside a multimillion-dollar project because it would hurt my feelings?" Jillian scoffed.

"Yes! I'm telling you, he cares about you."

"Even if he does—and I don't think that's the case, at least not the way you mean—but even if he does, he cares about his family more. When push comes to shove, he's going to do right by them, and if I get hurt in the process, well, that's simple collateral damage."

After all, family always came first, and she wasn't anyone's family.

Cold pizza and a lone beer of unknown age. The state of his refrigerator was pathetic. He could order some Chinese takeout, but he didn't want to wait for it. Resigned, he grabbed a slice and the longneck bottle.

Twisting off the top, he leaned a hip against the counter, content to eat standing up after ten hours hunched over a desk. This was not turning out to be a stellar Saturday.

He'd gotten into town yesterday morning and had spent the whole day in various meetings at Caruso headquarters. Today he'd been stuck at his desk, dealing with the inevitable paperwork that those meetings generated. Somehow, he'd managed to put off any questions about the Sandpiper, but he knew it was only a matter of time before his father would expect a status update. Burying himself in reports and sales figures was nothing more than the urban version of hiding his head in the sand. If he kept busy enough, he wouldn't have to think about how to handle the Sandpiper or, worse, how to handle Jillian.

He had tried calling her at least a dozen times in the past week, but had gotten her voice mail every time. She'd obviously started screening his calls, and it hurt more than he wanted to admit.

Hearing her voice, discussing his day with her, had become second nature. Somehow she'd become the person he bounced ideas around with, the person he went to for advice, or just a listening ear. Obviously she didn't feel the same way. He should have expected this. Once the grant proposal was denied, and despite their best efforts, he knew it probably would be, Caruso Hotels would buy the Sandpiper and Jillian Everett would kick him out of her life for good. Maybe she was just trying to do him a favor by ending their friendship, or whatever it was, now, before things got really ugly.

He understood her reasons for fighting against Caruso Hotels—hell, he was actually starting to agree with her. Which just made everything more complicated. His instinct was to fly down there, make her see him, but that was the last thing she seemed to want. Which left him standing here, alone, trying to figure out a way to go on with his life. Or, more accurately, get a life.

A check of his watch showed it wasn't even eight yet; he could still go out. He was young, single and had money to burn. A night out was just what he needed after yet another long week.

Before he could change his mind, he pulled his cell phone from his back pocket and dialed his brother. Damian was supposed to have gotten back from Florence sometime last week, but he'd been too busy to call and ask him about his trip. A lame excuse. Tonight he'd make it up to him. Buy him a drink and listen to all the ways European cooking was superior to anything in America.

Three rings in, Damian picked up. "Hey, wow, was wondering if you'd call. Are you in town?"

"Yeah, sorry… I've been busy. Got in yesterday and just came up for air."

"Dude, you work too much. Seriously, you've got to live a little."

"Agreed. Starting now. Want to meet me for some drinks at Dry?"

Damian was silent for several seconds. "You want to go have drinks? At a club? Who are you, and what have you done with my brother?"

"Ha, ha, very funny. What's wrong with wanting to go out on a Saturday night?"

"Nothing, bro. It's just not like you. But, yeah, I'm up for it. Meet you there in an hour?"

That should be plenty of time to shower, change and get a cab over to the trendy bar, named for its famously dry martinis. "Yeah, that works. See you soon."

He called down to the doorman to request a cab, then took a quick shower. The scruffy look was still fashionable, right? No need to shave. Searching his seldom-used closet, he found designer jeans and a button-down dress shirt. The owner of Dry, Andrew Bennet, was a family friend, so getting in wasn't an issue, but he didn't want to look out of place, either. Keys in hand, he headed out the door, ready for whatever the night might bring.

Nic made it to Dry before Damian, so he elbowed his way to the main bar and sent his brother a text to meet him there. Music pulsed from hidden speakers, enticing the more adventurous onto a dance floor commanding most of the exposed second level. Spotting the bartender, he ordered a scotch on the rocks and then surveyed the action. Lots of what were probably young professionals, looking to unwind after working way too many hours. And of course, lots of people looking to hook up, men as well as women. Skintight and low-cut seemed to be the trend of the day, the couture clothes designed to showcase bodies perfected by spin classes and personal trainers. He had never realized how frenetic it all was, with everyone rushing to cram as much fun as possible into the meager downtime their lean-in lifestyle permitted.

By the time Damian appeared at his elbow, he had an empty glass and a full-on headache. Damian placed his own drink order and motioned to Nic, asking if he was ready for another. "Sure." Maybe the booze would drown out the pounding in his skull. Had this place always been so loud?

"So why are we here?" Damian asked, skipping over the usual pleasantries.

"To drink." He tipped up his glass, taking a large swallow of the fiery liquid. "Why else?"

Damian's eyes roamed the room, then came to rest on a particularly well-endowed blonde enthusiastically sucking on a lime. "There are other reasons. Thought maybe you were ready to come off whatever self-imposed dry spell you've been on. This place is practically dripping with possibilities."

His brother had a point. There was no shortage of attractive women, including the bombshell doing the tequila shooters. He certainly could appreciate the display, but nothing about her or the other women that had attempted to make eye contact drew his interest. They were trying too hard, making him feel like a conquest, a prize to be won. Not that he could explain that to his brother, so he just shrugged. "Maybe."

Damian quirked up an eyebrow at that, but didn't comment, content to drink and listen to the music.

One hour and three drinks later, Nic's head was a bit fuzzy, so he was slow to react when a leggy redhead with surgically perfect features moved in a little too close. He had nothing against a bit of harmless flirting, but she seemed to have more ambitious goals in mind. When her roaming hands started heading south, he realized he'd had enough.

Turning to Damian, he shouted over the music, "I'm leaving." Damian looked questioningly at the handsy redhead, but shrugged and followed him out.

"What happened? She seemed into you."

"What she was into was my pants pocket, with her hand. She was trying to get a grip on the goods, if you get my drift."

"And?"

"And I like to know a girl's name before she starts massaging the family jewels. I'm old-fashioned that way."

"Damn, Mom was right. I hate it when she's right."

"What the heck are you talking about?"

"Mom. She said you'd fallen for someone, some girl down in Florida. That she had you going to church and everything."

Great. "I haven't fallen for anyone, not like that." He scowled, hoping to intimidate his younger brother into dropping this line of questioning.

Damian was undeterred. "She says that you talk to her all the time—that you even hung up on her so you could talk to this chick."

"It's business, that's all. I'm helping her with some real estate stuff." That the help he was giving was in direct opposition to the goals of Caruso Hotels didn't need to be mentioned. "And I didn't hang up on Mom, for crying out loud. I'd already talked to her for half an hour, so when Jillian called on Skype I told Mom I had to go."

"Skype? What is she, some kind of cybersex babe?"

Damian barely had the words out of his mouth before Nic had him shoved against the brick wall of the club, one arm across his throat. "Don't talk like that about her, understand?"

Damian, eyes wide, nodded, unwilling or unable to speak while his trachea was being crushed.

Nic stepped back, breathing hard. Crap, what was he doing? He scrubbed a hand over his jaw, feeling the bristles, taking the time to calm down and think clearly, or as clearly as the alcohol would let him. "Damian, I'm sorry, I had too much to drink, I shouldn't have—"

Damian's hoot of laughter cut him off. "Oh, boy, you

are totally messed up over this girl." His idiot brother was grinning from ear to ear. "No worries. I'll even be your best man, just let me know when the wedding is."

"Very funny." Great, if this got back to his parents, he'd be signed up for a tux fitting before he knew what hit him. "Like I said, she's just…" Hell, he didn't know. A friend? A colleague? The woman that kept him up at night, aching? "She's just someone I met. Besides, that's all over with. I haven't even talked to her since I was down there last week." Mainly because she wouldn't answer his phone calls.

"Wait, you saw her last week? I thought you were in Orlando last week?"

He was never drinking again. Ever. "Yeah, well, I drove over to Paradise Isle while I was there."

"Orlando to Paradise Isle? That's quite the booty call." Damian ducked this time; he was smaller and more sober, and easily eluded Nic's drunken punch. "Sorry, dude, that was just too easy."

"You're a jerk, you know that?"

"Yeah, I know. But I'll buy you a late dinner to soak up that booze, to make it up to you. Let's get out of here."

"Fine."

"Oh, and Nic?"

"Yeah?"

"Mom was definitely right." Nic glared, but didn't have a response, at least not one that Damian was going to buy. Not after seeing how riled up he got over a few remarks about Jillian. He was still hot about it, could still feel the temper simmering within him.

Which told him, more than Damian's taunts had, that his mom was right. He was really falling for Jillian. Maybe it was time he let her know it.

Chapter Twelve

A long afternoon at the beach with Murphy had scorched her skin but cleared her head. She'd even let Mollie talk her into dinner, and then drinks, at Pete's. Her canine buddy had been worn-out when she'd dropped him off, and now, climbing the stairs to her apartment, she felt about the same way. It was a good kind of tired, though, and she was glad she'd taken the time to catch up with Mollie. Sure, they saw each other at work every day, but it wasn't the same. Chatting with her friend had reminded her she had people in her life that cared, that she wasn't dependent on Nic Caruso or any man to keep her entertained.

After unlocking the door, she crossed the small living room and headed straight for the bathroom. She stripped off her tank top, shorts and bathing suit, leaving them in a pile on the floor, and turned the water on full force.

Nothing felt better than a hot, soapy shower after a day at the beach.

She took her time, using her favorite deep conditioner to rehydrate her curls after the salt water. A tingly, ginger-infused body wash got rid of the sticky sunscreen residue and left her feeling refreshed. She chose one of her biggest, softest bath towels for her body, and another for her hair. An orange-and-ginger-scented body lotion slathered on from head to toe finished her mini home spa treatment. She really should do this more often; she didn't need to wait for a big date to pamper herself a little. Feeling soft and pretty was its own reward.

A glance at her cat clock with the waggling tail told her it was already late, but after the beer she drank she should hydrate before going to bed. So she slipped into her favorite old nightshirt and went to the kitchen to pour a giant glass of water. Minutes later, she was perched on her hand-me-down couch, scanning the channels and sipping her drink. An old sitcom marathon was the best she could find, unless she wanted to watch endless infomercials for products she'd never heard of.

By the third episode her eyelids were sagging more than the punch lines. She really should go to bed, but getting off the couch sounded like a lot of work. Easier to just curl up right where she was. She snuggled farther into the cushions and snapped off the flickering television. Drifting off, she was in that lovely not-quite-asleep haze when the phone buzzed.

"Hello?" she managed to mumble, answering it without thinking to check the caller ID.

"Hi, Jillian. It's Nic. Did I wake you up? I didn't realize it was so late." His deep voice rumbled through the phone, a wakeup call to every sleeping nerve in her body.

"Um, no. I mean, well, not quite. I'm camped out on the couch and was just kind of dozing. Too lazy to get up and go to bed. I don't even know what time it is."

"Oh. It's almost midnight, I think. I shouldn't have called so late. I'll let you get back to sleep."

"No!" She scrambled to a sitting position. Now that she could hear his voice, she wanted him to keep talking, to ignore all the reasons she'd been avoiding his calls. "No, I'm awake. Really, it's fine. What's up? Did you hear something about the grant?"

"The grant? No, not yet. I'm sure you'll hear something soon."

"Hopefully." Why did he call if it wasn't about the grant? Did he just want to torture her, string her along a little longer?

"Yeah. Hopefully."

The silence echoed, stretching her nerves until she couldn't take it any longer. Maybe she would regret asking, but she had to know. "Nic?"

"Yeah?" His soft, husky voice sounded only inches from her ear, tempting her heart into wishing for things that weren't there.

"Why did you call?" Breath held, she waited.

"Because—well, I just wanted to talk to you, but you've been kind of hard to get ahold of lately. I care about you, you know."

Guilt formed a knot in her throat. Swallowing past it, she forced some cheer into her voice. "Oh, I'm fine. Went to the beach today with Mollie. I took Murphy. You should see him chase the ball in the waves. He's a real fiend about it."

"Yeah, I bet that's something." He cleared his throat. "In fact, when I come down there, maybe—"

"Maybe what, Nic?" Her embarrassment and guilt fused into anger in the space of a heartbeat. "Maybe when you're down here directing the demolition of the Sandpiper, you'll find some time to hang out on the beach? Show me where you're going to put in the first high-rise, and the water park, and who knows what else? Maybe you can take me on a tour this time, show me the new and improved vision for Paradise Isle, with all the tacky T-shirt shops and after-hours nightclubs? Is that what you think, Nic?"

His words were low and controlled when he spoke. "I wasn't thinking anything of the kind, Jillian."

"Good! Because I don't think anything of you or your plans to ruin the only home I've ever known." She was sobbing now, her voice cracking. "So stop pretending we're friends, or that you're going to come down here and we'll have some kind of romantic reunion, you, me and Murphy. Stop acting like you care, and stop calling me." She pressed the end-call button and threw down the phone, mortified.

Where did that come from? Hadn't she told Mollie just this afternoon that she agreed with Nic's motives, if not his plans? And yet here she was, throwing it all in his face, acting like a crazy woman. Because he was going to destroy the Sandpiper?

Or because he was going to destroy her heart?

Was she angry with him or with herself for letting her guard down, letting someone in?

Not that it mattered. That display of theatrics was guaranteed to keep him out of her life. Too bad it was a bit too late. No matter what she told her friends, this pain in her heart could only mean one thing. Somehow, she'd managed to fall in love with Nic Caruso, a man destined to destroy her world, and her life.

Sunday was usually Nic's chance to sleep in, at least on the days he didn't have an early flight. And since he'd lain awake for hours last night, trying to puzzle out his disastrous phone call to Jillian, he really needed the extra rest. A detail that his sister Isabella didn't care about in the least. When he'd ignored her phone call, she had just sweet-talked the doorman into letting her in. At least that's what she said. Eyeing his take-no-prisoners sister, he figured she'd most likely bulldozed whatever unlucky man had gotten in her way.

Right now she was standing in his dining room, towering over him while he slowly drank a cup of much-needed coffee. She was wearing jeans and a tailored blouse instead of her usual designer suit, but she still oozed the kind of confident power that had made her successful in the male-dominated world of investment banking. But if she thought that kind of power play was going to work on him, she was sorely mistaken.

"I'm assuming there is a reason you barged in so early?"

"It's only early to people that were up late getting drunk."

Great. Damian didn't waste any time tattling. "It wasn't that late, and I wasn't drunk." At least the first part was true; he had been home at a decent hour.

"You were drunk enough to shove Damian around."

"Since when do I need to be drunk to want to mess around with Damian?" He certainly felt like beating on his brother right now. How much had he told her?

"Okay, you have a point." Dropping the tough interrogation act, she sat down next to him, her golden eyes filled with concern. "But seriously, what's going on with you?"

Oh, boy. He could stand up to her tough-girl talk all day long, but he couldn't resist his sisters when they turned mushy. "Listen, it's not a big deal, okay? Some girl hit on me at the club, and I turned her down."

"Why?"

What, did all his siblings think he was some kind of playboy? Was turning down a girl that earthshaking? "No real reason, she just didn't do it for me."

"Maybe." She watched him closely; she had always been too perceptive for her own good. "Or maybe she was the wrong girl. Maybe there's someone else you're interested in."

"Yeah, well, sometimes the right girl is still all wrong," he muttered, shoveling in another bit of cereal.

"Aha! So there is a girl. Okay, well, by 'wrong,' do you just mean it might take some actual effort on your part? 'Cause, big brother, I have to tell you, you have gotten lazy."

He nearly choked on his cornflakes. Lazy? She had to be kidding.

"Don't you look at me that way, Dominic Caruso. I know you work hard, but when it comes to women, you've never had to lift a finger. They just throw themselves at you, and the most you have had to do is decide which one you want. I'm betting that for once, you've found one that won't come running when you snap your fingers. Am I right?"

He didn't want her to be right. He definitely didn't like the picture she was painting of him, but there was some truth to her words. "Let's just say that when I tried to talk to her last night, she hung up on me, crying."

Isabella's smug smile seemed completely out of place. "Oh, that's nothing. Just give her some flowers and grovel. Totally fixable."

"I don't think it's that easy."

"That's because you've never really groveled. Trust me, it works." The glint in her eyes told him she'd seen her share of such men.

"There's more to it than that. There are other…complications."

"So tell me about them. You know you're dying to tell someone. And unlike Damian, I won't go running my mouth to the rest of the family."

That much was true. Isabella's brain was like a vault. Nothing spilled out without her express permission. And maybe talking it out would help him to make sense of things. Drinking hadn't. So he explained, as best he could, the situation, telling her about the town, Jillian, the Sandpiper and Caruso's plans to transform the island. By the end of his story, his sister had tears in her eyes and a sappy smile on her face. "What? Why are you looking at me like that?"

"Because it's so romantic," she gushed, fanning her face to stop the tears from ruining her makeup.

"It's not romantic, it's a mess." Standing, he carried his dishes to the kitchen, loading them into the dishwasher with more force than necessary.

"Well, yeah, it's a mess. But it's romantic, too. The two of you are star-crossed lovers, like Romeo and Juliet."

"And look how they ended up."

"Okay, bad example. But seriously, it has to be fate

that the two of you met. If you really have feelings for her, if you love her, you have to find a way. You can't let anything stop you."

"Whoa…who said anything about love?" He staggered back, knocked off-kilter by the idea. "We've only known each other a few weeks, nowhere near long enough to be throwing the *L* word around."

"Oh, yeah?" Isabella advanced on him, coming in for the kill. "And exactly how long did Mom and Dad know each other before they got married?"

"Three weeks." *Oh, man.* "But that was…different."

"Not so different. And you know they're just as much in love now as they were then."

Nodding, he rubbed his chest, struggling to even out his breathing. His parents *were* very happy, but he'd always thought their whirlwind romance was the exception to the rule. Certainly nothing that could happen to him. His father was undeniably a risk taker in every facet of his life. A whirlwind romance, a risky business idea: that was Lorenzo Caruso's modus operandi. Nic, on the other hand, was methodical to the bone.

Someday he'd planned on falling in love, preferably with someone he was already friendly with, and only after a long courtship. They'd date casually at first, then more seriously, then after a year or so announce an engagement at just the right time. That was the right way to go about things.

Isabella interrupted his tumbling thoughts with a dilemma of her own. "I actually didn't come by here just to give you a hard time. I wanted to ask you to put out some feelers for me."

"You're looking for a new job?" He knew she'd been

under a lot of stress, working longer hours than even he did, but he hadn't thought she was that unhappy.

"Yeah, it's time. I took this position as a stepping stone, a chance to get experience in a big company. But I'm tired of doing grunt work. The pay is great, but I want a chance to make real decisions. Instead, I'm spending all my hours crunching numbers, just for some executive to ignore them and do whatever he wants, anyway. I need a new challenge, a different way to use my skills. Maybe something with some travel. I've always envied you, getting to stay in all sorts of interesting places, meeting new people. Me? My biggest adventure is getting a new flavor of nondairy creamer for my coffee."

"It's not all glamorous, trust me."

"Nothing is, but I didn't come here to complain, just to ask you to keep an ear out. Let me know if you hear of anything that sounds interesting."

"Sure, I can do that. I don't have a lot of contacts in finance, but if you're looking for a change, there are lots of businesses that would jump at a chance to have someone with your experience. It's just a matter of who has openings."

"Thanks, I know it will take some time. Just fix your woman problems, and by then I'll probably have my dream job all lined up." As confident of her success as ever, she let herself out, leaving him alone with his thoughts. And if any of what she'd accused him of was true, he had plenty of thinking to do.

Chapter Thirteen

Jillian regretted her angry outburst at Nic, but what had her nerves twanging like a tautly strung banjo wasn't the fight, it was discovering how deep her feelings for him ran. He might think he was interested right now, but she was realistic enough to know that any feelings he had couldn't last, not long-term. Anyone could see they were all wrong for each other. Even without the controversy over the Sandpiper, there were so many reasons they could never work as a couple. He was a rolling stone, constantly traveling. She was a homebody, with a need to plant deep roots. He was wealthy, with powerful family connections. She was happy to finally be able to afford rent and her own car. And of course, his life centered on his family, and she was an orphan who didn't know the first thing about those kinds of blood bonds.

Added all up, it equaled disaster. And yet, somehow

she'd managed to fall for him, anyway. Hook, line and sinker. The only bright point was that he didn't know how she felt. In fact, after that last phone call, he probably assumed she hated him. Better that than to face humiliation on top of rejection. This way she could nurse her wounded heart in peace, with no one the wiser. Surely, after a while, it would heal. She'd lived through worse. She'd live through this, too.

Her coping strategy of the moment was to spend time with Murphy, her wannabe dog. She'd increased her training sessions with him, and he was really turning into an obedient little guy. He loved the extra attention, and she found comfort in his furry friendship. Mrs. Rosenberg had asked a few times about Nic, but when Jillian refused to talk about him, she had backed off. Even Cassie and Mollie had stopped asking about him, instead focusing on the future of the Sandpiper and Paradise Isle. The first thing anyone asked when they saw her was if she'd heard about the grant decision yet. The stress of waiting for news was almost worse than the heartbreak over Nic. Almost.

Arriving home after another long day at work and then an hour working with Murphy, she was ready to call it a night. Out of habit she stopped at the row of metal mailboxes, using her tiny key to access a stack of what looked like bills and junk mail. Shoving them in her purse, she climbed the stairs to her second-floor apartment, trying to decide on dinner. Sandwich? Soup? What the heck? Might as well have both.

Once inside, she tossed her purse and mail on the kitchen counter, the envelopes fanning out across the tan Formica. She found a can of alphabet soup and heated it up on the stove, letting it simmer while she made a quick ham sandwich. Cooking didn't seem worth it when there was no one to cook for, so this would have to do.

She ladled the soup into a bowl and started nibbling the sandwich, sitting at the breakfast bar that extended from the counter. Too tired to read, she let her mind wander. She ought to wash her car this weekend. Organize the pantry. Oh, and clean out the mail basket; there were ads and coupons and bills all mixed together in a jumble. She had a tendency to just pile it up, and then she didn't have the coupons when she wanted them, and it was a pain to find the bills and pay them. Really, she should start that now. Go through the stuff she'd just dropped on the table, sort it out. It would at least be a start.

She put her dishes in the sink and scooped up the scattered mail, taking it to her desk in the entryway. Pulling out the wastebasket she kept under the desk, she began sorting. Advertisement, bill, craft store coupon, bill, political brochure and a plain brown envelope with the State of Florida seal on it. Her hands trembled. Maybe she shouldn't open it. Maybe she should give it to the Island Preservation Society, let them open it.

"Don't be such a baby," she scolded herself, ripping open the envelope before she could chicken out again. She unfolded the single page, holding her breath as she quickly scanned the typewritten lines. *We regret to inform you...*

None of the other words made sense after that, or even mattered. There would be no grant money. The city wouldn't be able to purchase the inn; it wouldn't be listed as an historic place. It would be torn down, and in its place would be some mega-resort with everything the busy traveler could want—for a price. They'd overrun the beaches, crowd the streets and take over the restaurants. The Paradise Isle she'd come to love would no longer be the quiet sanctuary of her dreams. And there was absolutely nothing she, or anyone else, could do about it.

Sinking to the floor, she tucked her head against her knees and let the tears come. She cried for the sheer ugliness of what was going to happen, for the upheaval sure to come, but mostly for the loss of yet one more place, one more dream. Would she ever find a safe haven of her own?

A good cry helped to wash the pain out of head and heart, leaving an empty numbness in its place. Soon, she'd have to figure out the details and set up a meeting of the Island Preservation Society to break the bad news. For now, though, there was an even bigger hurdle to clear. She needed to let Nic know. And then face the consequences, whatever they were. She was sure he'd be nice about it, of course. He didn't want to hurt her, of that she was sure. But hurt her he would, and she couldn't even work up any righteous anger about it.

As much as she hated what he was going to do, deep down she admired his devotion to his family, his loyalty. She couldn't ask him to betray the trust his family had placed in him when they brought him into the company. Which meant that there was nothing left to do but move on and make the best of it.

Unfolding herself from her cramped position on the floor, she stood tall, bracing herself for the coming conversation. She needed to be strong—she wouldn't, couldn't, let him hear her pain. No, she'd be professional, impart the information he needed, and that would be the end of her dealings with Nic Caruso.

She dialed with steady hands, calming herself through

sheer force of will. She could do this. The phone rang.
Her stomach flopped. She hadn't talked to him since
their big fight. What if he didn't want to talk to her,
wouldn't answer? Another ring. Just as she lost her nerve
and started to hang up, he answered.

"Jillian?" He sounded cautious, but not angry. That
was a good sign. At least he wasn't going to hang up
on her.

"Hi, Nic. I'm sure you're wondering why I'm calling.
And I won't keep you. I just wanted to inform you that
I received a letter from the State Registry of Historical
Places, and they were not able to grant us any funds."

"Oh."

She tried to finish quickly, get it over with. "So, just
thought you should know, so you can make arrangements, do whatever it is you do. So anyway—"

"Hey, listen, for what it's worth, I'm sorry."

She didn't want to hear that. She wasn't going to be
able to hold it together if he started pitying her. "Well,
be that as it may, the fact of the matter is, you win. You
get what you want."

"Jillian, I need to talk to you—"

She hung up. She'd told him what she had to tell
him; she wasn't going to torture herself by staying on
the line, making small talk, pretending things were just
fine between them. How could she? He had stolen from
her the one thing she'd come to count on: her home. She
had wanted to raise a family here, on the quiet and safe
streets she'd grown to love. But now those streets would
be overrun with tourists, the small shops replaced with
chain stores and after-hours nightclubs. She'd lived in
other places where tourism had taken over, and had no
desire to repeat the experience. She knew some people

thrived on the hustle and bustle, but she craved peace and a sense of community that those busy cities couldn't provide.

And, beneath that hurt, there was a deeper, sharper pain, one that tore at her battered heart.

How could it hurt this much to lose a man she should never have fallen for in the first place?

Chapter Fourteen

As much as Nic had come to dislike the constant traveling his job required, he had never actually dreaded a trip before. Of course, it had never been so personal before. Boarding the plane to Florida, all he'd been able to think about was Jillian and how badly he'd messed things up. Not that he could think of a different way to have handled things, other than never meeting her at all. He couldn't have prevented the bond that had formed between them any more than he could prevent his next breath. Heaven knew he'd tried. But she'd gotten stuck inside him somehow, and now he was trapped, forced to either hurt the woman he wanted to protect or betray the man that had given him everything. He couldn't do that to his father.

So his only option was to try to minimize the impact of the hotel on the island and hope that would be enough to show Jillian how he felt. It wouldn't be easy, and most of the changes couldn't be prevented. But he had to try. He only hoped that would be enough for Jillian to forgive him. Maybe then he'd have a chance with her. It wasn't a great plan, but what else could he do?

The flight, for once, felt too short. In what seemed like no time he was loading his luggage into yet another rental car. The motions were familiar, but the anxiety chewing through his gut was not. He'd always been a confident person, and years in the field had assured him he had the skills needed to complete the task at hand. So it wasn't fear of failure that nagged him now. It was the cold, hard fact that this time, he didn't want to succeed.

Shrugging off his melancholy mood, he concentrated on navigating the horrendous traffic that Orlando was famous for. Caruso Hotels would definitely have to arrange for some kind of shuttle from the airport, so vacationers didn't show up to the resort already in a bad mood. Maybe even a helicopter service for the VIP guests; they'd love that. The noise would be an issue, but in the scheme of things, the prestige would be worth it. He'd send a memo to the development team so they could work a landing pad into their plans. Focusing on the details let him avoid thinking about the ramifications of what he was about to do.

That strategy worked well until he approached the spot where he'd rescued Murphy, and all the memories of that first weekend came flooding back in Technicolor clarity. Her gentle touch with the injured dog, her eyes so big and blue, her lips and how right they'd felt on his own. Just thinking about it had his body responding, his blood pressure rising.

Damn, if he was this wound up just thinking about

her, how much harder was it going to be to see her? And
he was going to see her. Even if he couldn't convince
her of his feelings, he didn't want to end things like they
had, with her angry and hanging up on him. He wanted
a chance to explain, to apologize, to tell her his plans to
make the transition as easy as possible. And, if he was
honest with himself, he just couldn't stay away.

Which was why he found himself climbing her staircase as dusk was falling, knowing she would, most
likely, slam the door in his face. When his knock was
met with silence his first assumption was that she was,
in fact, avoiding him. It was only when he scanned the
parking lot and didn't find her car that he realized his
mistake. She was probably taking her nightly run with
Murphy; he'd somehow forgotten her commitment to the
pet she couldn't have. He could sit and wait for her, but
his growling stomach gave him a better idea.

There was a diner around the corner; he could pick
up food for the both of them, a peace offering of sorts.
Deciding to walk rather than drive, he once again noted
the Norman Rockwell quality of the town. Everywhere
he looked, he saw kids playing in the twilight, families gathering in neat little houses, older folks rocking
on front porches, as they probably had every evening
for decades, watching the comings and goings of their
neighborhood.

Even Mary's Diner was picturesque in its own way,
a throwback to the 1950s, with red booths and chrome
accents everywhere. A few single men sat at the bar;
the tables were filled mostly with young families grabbing a bite out after a busy day. The service was quick
and friendly. A matronly woman wearing a frilly apron
took his order, and within minutes he had two meat loaf

dinners and a lemon pound cake packed up and ready to go. The aromas tantalized him as he made his way back; hopefully she'd be hungry enough to let him in, at least long enough to eat.

She arrived a few minutes after he did, pulling into the parking lot directly across from where he sat at her front door. He knew the minute she saw him; her eyes narrowed, as if just the sight of him caused her pain.

What had he been thinking, coming here?

It was too late now. He only hoped he could reassure her somehow, make things even a little bit right for her. Because as much as he knew he should just walk away, he couldn't do it. Not yet.

The last thing Jillian had expected when she finally got home that night was Nic Caruso at her door. They had no business left to discuss, and she thought she'd hinted pretty clearly that she wanted no personal contact with him, either. Obviously subtlety was lost on him. She'd just have to tell him, politely but firmly, to go. Whatever he thought he wanted, he wasn't going to get it from her. She wasn't equipped to deal with the emotional maelstrom he triggered—she was too raw. The sooner she got him out of her life, she sooner she could pick up the pieces of her broken heart.

When she had stomped up the last step, she saw the bags of food. Damn him. She was starving; no way was she going to turn down food from Mary's. Fine, they'd eat—quickly—and then he could leave. Whatever he had to say, he'd have to say fast, before she finished devouring whatever was behind that wonderful aroma.

She refused to ask him why he was there as she pushed past him to open the door. It didn't matter, anyway. "Put the food on the counter. I'll get plates and drinks."

He did as she instructed, opening up Styrofoam containers to reveal savory meat loaf, mashed potatoes and carrots. Her stomach rumbled, betraying her interest in his culinary olive branch. She assumed that's what it was, and it annoyed her that it had worked. Just having him in her apartment was a major mistake, one she wouldn't have made if she had been thinking with her head instead of her stomach. The irony was that now that she'd seen him, the only thing she had an appetite for was him.

Get a grip. She couldn't let him see how much she wanted him. She couldn't lose her pride on top of her heart.

She forced herself to set the plates down on the breakfast bar rather than slam them, not wanting to show more emotion than necessary. Crossing to the refrigerator, she considered the options, then closed it again and grabbed a bottle of red wine off the counter. A little liquid courage to get her through this. She silently handed him the bottle and corkscrew, then fetched the wineglasses. He poured generously, then clinked his glass against hers. "Salute."

She looked up, unfamiliar with the toast, and her eyes met his over the raised glasses. She read regret there, and concern, emotions a little too close to pity, and she wouldn't be pitied. Not again. She'd gotten over being the poor little orphan girl long ago, and didn't need him feeling sorry for her. He might as well pour salt on her wounds.

"So, I assume you're here to buy the Sandpiper, tie up all the loose ends or whatever. Then you'll be off to your next conquest." *Soon*, she added silently. The sooner he was gone, the sooner she could try to forget the way he made her feel. Even now, knowing what he was here to do, she found herself wanting to let down her guard, recapture the closeness that had sprung up so quickly between them.

"Not just yet. I need to schedule more land surveys, have various inspections done, that kind of thing. And I'm going to order an environmental survey, as well. It isn't strictly required, since the zoning won't change, but I'm going to do my best to limit the impact to the beaches and wildlife. I want to make this work, and I want to do right by Paradise Isle. I want to do right by you."

"So that's why you're here?" She gestured to the apartment around her. "You came to my home, knowing how I feel about all this, to tell me it won't be so bad, after all?" She didn't know if she should laugh or cry at his brazenness.

"Well, yeah. And to bring you dinner." He smiled cockily, melting her defenses in the space of a heartbeat.

"That was a dirty trick." But she took a bite of the meat loaf, anyway. She *was* hungry, and heaven help her, she couldn't keep up the bitch act around him. She liked him too much. Liked him? Who was she kidding? She was head over heels for him. Just watching him sit in her kitchen, in faded jeans and an old band T-shirt that stretched enticingly when he moved, had her hormones working on overdrive.

But it was more than his looks; it was who he was as a person that had gotten her to let down her guard. Even when they should have been enemies, they still slipped into the easy banter that had become so natural between them. She loved hearing about the exotic places he had traveled, and he always seemed genuinely interested in the stories she told him about the animals at work. They'd found they also shared similar views on politics, religion and literature, but were, of course, rivals in football and baseball. His family was another frequent topic of conversation, one that often had her crying tears of laughter as he told stories of his childhood.

"Is Damian back yet from Florence?" she asked, reaching for more wine.

He filled her glass, and topped off his own. "Yeah, he got back a few weeks ago, even more arrogant than he was before."

She grinned. A certain level of self-confidence was a trait the brothers shared, whether Nic acknowledged it or not. "So I take it you got a chance to see him the last time you were home?" With his crazy schedule, he didn't always get time for family visits on his brief trips to New York.

"Um, yeah…sure, I saw him," Nic mumbled, suddenly very interested in the last few carrots on his plate.

"What? What happened?" She smelled a story here. When he didn't answer, she grabbed his arm, spinning his bar stool toward her. Facing him, she demanded, "Spill it!"

"Nothing happened, really. I had a few drinks and, well, things got a little tense. But it's fine now, no big deal."

Jillian had heard enough about the family to know that a scuffle between the brothers was nothing new. But something about his reaction had her curiosity piqued. "What was the fight about?"

Again, he didn't answer. Now she had to know. She

slid off her stool into the space between them. Taking his face in her hands, she pulled him down so she could look into his eyes. "Hey, seriously, what started it this time?"

Sighing, he knocked back the rest of his wine. "It was just a misunderstanding. He was trying to get a rise out of me, and it worked. I mentioned that you and I had been talking on Skype a lot, and he insinuated I was using you for cybersex."

Speechless, she felt the blood rise in her cheeks. She wasn't a prude, but wow, she hadn't expected that. Unbidden, seductive images streaked across her mind's eye.

"Don't worry. I made it clear to him that's not the situation. At all."

"That's…good." Suddenly she realized how close she was standing to him; only inches separated them. There wasn't enough oxygen, not enough space. She needed more distance, physically and emotionally. She tried to clear her suddenly dry throat. "Obviously that's not the kind of thing that would happen with us."

"Oh, I don't know," he answered, reaching out to brush a stray curl from her face. "I can't say the idea *never* occurred to me."

Her mouth parted in shock and Nic took full advantage of the offering, lowering his lips to hers, tasting, testing, gently seducing. His tenderness was her undoing. Time stopped, the world spun away. Distantly, she knew this shouldn't happen, but there was no way she could stop it. Nothing else mattered, just him. Just this moment and this man.

He'd never paid much attention to descriptions of heaven, but it couldn't be better than this. She was warm and soft in his arms; her lips were a silken seduction tempting him to explore and linger. Holding himself back, ignoring the fire in his body that demanded to be fed, was like holding back a raging river. It took all his willpower but he kept his touch light, sampling rather than devouring the mouth she so innocently offered up for him.

When his resolve was strained nearly to the breaking point, he forced himself to pull away. Panting, he leaned his forehead against hers. "I didn't expect that."

Her eyes were glazed, but she shuttered them quickly, turning away at his words. "I'm sorry." Her voice trembled, plucking at his guilt.

When she tried to walk away, he grabbed her arm, stopping her. "Don't be sorry—I'm not."

Shaking him off, she pulled out of his grip, backing into the living room, putting as much space between them as was possible in the small apartment. "This can't keep happening." Her eyes pleaded with him, pain reflecting in the smoky depths.

"It can, if you'll just let it." He shoved his hands through his hair. "Damn it, I can't force you to admit what you feel, but I'm done hiding how I feel. And I'm sure as hell not to pretend I'm sorry, that I regret kissing you. And I don't think you regret it, either."

"I think you should go now." Her arms were wrapped around her body, her gaze refusing to meet his.

"Don't do this. I know you want—"

"What I want is for you to go." Her voice cracked with emotion. "Please…just go."

Damn it. Look at what he was doing to her. He'd been a fool to think he could see her and keep his hands off her. All he'd wanted was to make things a bit better, a bit easier for her. Instead, he'd made of mess of everything, leaving her worse off than before. But he'd told her the truth; he didn't regret that kiss, or any of the others for that matter. He only regretted hurting her. His instinct had been to protect her, but for now the best way to do that was to leave.

"I'll go." He'd brought nothing with him other than the food; there was nothing to collect, no way to stall on his way to the door she held open for him. He wanted to stay and fight, to make her let him stay, but the tears spilling onto her cheeks stopped him when no argument or harsh word would have.

"Goodbye. And Nic? Please don't come back."

Her final words haunted him as he drove through the night. He had reserved a room at the Sandpiper, but he took the highway back to Orlando instead. He didn't trust himself to stay away with so little distance between them. Even now, knowing how badly he'd hurt her, he had to fight to keep from turning around and forcing her to let him back in.

Maybe he'd been wrong about them, about making it work. She obviously wasn't going to forgive him. And he didn't blame her; he'd attacked the one thing she held dear—her community.

Being without her might kill him, but if seeing him was going to hurt her, then the only solution was to leave the island, leave the project. He'd have to find someone else to take over; there was no way he could be there, day after day, and not see her, even if only accidentally. He'd never walked away from an assignment before, but right now his reputation was the least of his worries. He'd turn over his notes to one of the up-and-coming executives, give them a chance to prove themselves. He could spin it that way, make it sound like he was mentoring someone, helping them move up in the ranks.

His father would be a hard sell, but certainly by now he'd earned some discretion. The project would go forward, and Jillian would get the space she'd asked for. He should have done this weeks ago, as soon as he started getting involved with her. But he'd always managed to keep his business and personal lives separate before; he hadn't expected it to be a problem.

But there was no way to compartmentalize his feelings for Jillian. She permeated every facet of his life; he'd even started dreaming about her. Right now he should be thinking about work, about finding the right person to take over the project, and figuring out how to streamline any collaboration. Instead, he kept seeing the tears on her face, each one another slice at his soul.

He'd dated dozens of beautiful women, so why did this one bring him to his knees?

The answer was obvious. He was in love with her. Only he'd figured it out way too late.

Furious with himself, with fate, his job, he pounded his fist on the steering wheel, relishing the sting. Physical pain faded quickly. Much worse was this throbbing ache in his chest, threatening to consume him. Maybe with some distance he'd be thinking more clearly and would find a way out of this mess. Because the alternative was unthinkable.

Chapter Fifteen

Jillian knocked quietly on Cassie's door, not wanting to wake Emma if she was already asleep. What time did four-year-olds go to bed, anyway? Not that she knew what time it was. She'd spent longer than she should have indulging in tears after Nic left, then had gone on a cleaning spree, taking her angst out on her kitchen. She now had gleaming tile and the beginnings of a plan. Talking to Cassie was the first step to putting it in motion.

Her friend opened the door, ushering her into the small but cheery 1950s cottage she'd purchased when Emma was born. Soft throw rugs were scattered on the terrazzo floor, creating a welcoming and child-friendly space. Family photos and pictures of various pets intermingled with books on the large, built-in bookcases, the only real decoration other than a few jewel-toned throw cushions. Jillian kicked off her shoes at the door and sat cross-legged on the taupe microfiber couch. Cassie joined her, settling slightly sideways so she could face her friend.

"Thanks for letting me in, I know it's probably late. I hope I didn't wake Emma."

"You know you can come by anytime. And Emma sleeps like a rock—a five-piece band wouldn't wake her up. But it is late, at least for you, so I assume it's important."

Jillian took a deep breath, steadying her nerves. She'd practiced a speech on the way over here, but now it seemed so scripted. Maybe she should just lay it all out there, and then deal with the aftermath. "I'd like to tender my notice of resignation."

"Excuse me? What did you just say? I must have misheard. I would have sworn you just said you were quitting."

"That's exactly what I'm saying. I've stayed in Paradise a long time, longer than anywhere else I've lived. I stayed because of the kind of place it is, but that's all changing, so there's no reason I shouldn't move on, try something new."

Cassie narrowed her brow. "Funny, I would have thought your best friends being here might be a reason to stick around."

Crap. She didn't want to offend Cassie, but she had to move. She couldn't stay in Paradise with Nic parading in and out of town constantly. And once the resort was built it would be a constant reminder. She would never be able to put him behind her if she stayed here.

Maybe she just wasn't meant to have a real home. Some people never settled down; they moved whenever the urge hit them. Just because she'd always dreamed of putting down roots didn't mean it was the right thing or that this was the right place. She knew better than most that dreams didn't always come true. "I love you guys, you know that. But just because I won't live here doesn't mean we can't still be friends. I'll call, we can talk on Skype, email, text. And when I'm settled you can come visit me."

"Settled where?" Cassie threw her hands up in the air. "Do you even know where you want to go?"

She'd anticipated that question. Unfortunately, she hadn't come up with an answer yet. "Not yet. But I will. I'm going to start checking ads, see who's hiring. Maybe try somewhere up north for a change."

"So let me get this straight." Cassie had shifted to what Jillian thought of as her doctor voice. "You have no idea where you want to go, nothing planned out, and yet you are quitting your job—a job I was reasonably sure you liked—leaving your best friends, and deserting the town you love. And you are doing this why?"

"When Caruso Hotels buys the Sandpiper—"

"Ah, Caruso, that's what this is about. Nic Caruso, to be specific. Damn him. What happened? If he hurt you, I know how to castrate—"

"That won't be necessary." She managed a smile at the image, pleased by the show of solidarity if not the dramatic suggestion. "He didn't do anything, really. Other than be the wrong man at the wrong time." She needed Cassie to understand. "He came by tonight. He's in town to start negotiations to buy the Sandpiper. He wanted to tell me he was sorry things turned out this way, that he would try to make the transition as painless as possible, even though we both know there isn't much he can do to minimize the impact of thousands of new tourists." She focused on her hands, resting them carefully in her lap. "He brought me dinner."

"What a bastard," Cassie said drolly.

Jillian continued without pause. "We talked, and for a while it was like before. Then it got…tense, sort of. And then he kissed me."

"And?"

"And it was wonderful, okay? The best kiss I've ever had. But then I stopped it. I can't go there when I know it can't work, not long-term." She swiped angrily at her eyes, refusing to cry over him anymore. "I get that he has to do his job, has to build the hotel. I fell in love with him, anyway. I'll find a way to get over him, but I can't keep seeing him. It hurts too much." Her voice cracked, but she didn't break down this time. No more. She'd learned to be strong a long time ago, and no man was going to break her. Not even Nic Caruso.

"Oh, Jillian…I'm so sorry."

"Don't feel sorry for me, okay? Just help me move on. Accept my resignation."

Cassie started to say something, then stopped. Getting up, she moved to the desk in the corner where she kept her computer. "Well, come on. Let's start searching those job databases. We need to find you somewhere fantastic, somewhere fun for me to visit."

Nic sat in one of the leather chairs facing the oak desk where his father conducted all his business. He'd waited until the end of the day to approach him, not wanting to chance their conversation being interrupted. Even still, he'd found Lorenzo Caruso tied up in a conference call with the marketing department.

Tapping his fingers on the leather, he took another swallow of the whiskey he'd helped himself to, trying to contain his nerves. He was generally given free rein with business decisions; as a vice president, he technically didn't need approval to hand off the Paradise Isle project. But his father would be curious, and it was better to head off any questions, rather than be put on the defensive later. At least, that was the plan.

His father waved a finger at him, signaling he would only be another minute. Good: the sooner this was over, the sooner he could get to work on something else, anything else. A new place, a new challenge—that was what he needed. Hopefully Dad would have something ready for him, something meaty that would take all his concentration. Something to get his mind off his impossible situation with Jillian.

Finally, his father hung up the phone, circling the desk to envelop Nic in a crushing hug. "What are you doing here? I didn't think I'd see you until next week!"

He returned the embrace, happier to see his father than he would have expected. The older man returned to his desk, settling on the edge of it rather than sitting behind it.

"Were there any problems?"

"No problems, Dad. As expected, the grant I told you about didn't go through, so there's no issue there. In fact, it should be a straightforward enough project that I'm going to have Mike Patrullo head this one up. He's been doing good work, and I think it would be a positive experience for him."

His father pursed his lips, swirling his own, mostly empty glass of whiskey, the golden liquid dancing in the light. "You've never turned an assignment of this magnitude over to someone else before."

"No, but this seemed like a good time to try it, let someone else take their shot."

"And this decision wouldn't have anything to do with a young lady your mother was telling me about, would it?"

Great. Was his whole family obsessed with his love life?

"And don't go blaming your mother. You know she just wants you to be happy," his father added before Nic could voice a complaint.

Cornered and not willing to lie to his father, he conceded the point. "Yeah, I guess it does have to do with her. I messed things up, badly."

"So you're running away? I thought I raised you better than that."

"I'm not running. She asked me to leave. Staying there would just make things harder for her, and—"

"And you're willing to make a sacrifice if it means you can help her out, is that right?"

"Yes." He relaxed a bit more into the buttery leather; he should have known his father would understand. He might be a savvy businessman, but he had raised his boys to be gentlemen, as well.

"Do you love her?"

The blunt question ripped through his careful posturing, resurrecting the headache he'd almost managed to forget about. Knowing his father wouldn't leave it alone, he gave the only answer he could. "Yes." Dropping his head back, he closed his eyes against the overhead lighting. "But that doesn't seem to matter."

"Dominic, love is the only thing that does matter."

Those were not the words he'd expected to hear from his ambitious father.

"You don't understand. She deserves things I can't give her. She needs someone that wants the same things as her, someone that can be there day in and day out, home for dinner, with kids and a dog in the backyard."

"Ah, I see." His father rested his hands together, steepling his fingers. "And that's not the kind of life you want."

"No. I mean, I don't know. But either way, it's not the life I have. Heck, I'm barely home long enough to read my mail, let alone have a relationship."

"True. And after investing so much time and effort into your work, you wouldn't want to change things now."

"It's not about what I want. It's about what needs to be done. I've got responsibilities. You know that—you're the one that taught me about responsibility."

"Yes, I did. And I've always been proud of your work ethic. But maybe I didn't do a very good job of teaching you about priorities."

"What's that supposed to mean? I should just drop everything, run off to Florida because I met a pretty girl?"

"No, not if that's all she is. But this isn't about playing beach blanket bingo with some random girl, is it?"

Nic shook his head, then got up and walked to one of the large windows overlooking the street far below. From this distance, the frantic pushing and shoving of evening commuters looked almost choreographed. Were any of them as twisted up inside as he was?

His father stepped up behind him. "You won't find the answers out there, son, and I don't have them, either. You're going to have to do some hard thinking. But

I trust you to find your way in this, just as you have in everything else."

Nic stayed at the window long after his father left, hoping for some inspiration in the place where so many pivotal decisions had been made.

A knock at the door found Jillian elbow deep in a box of books, trying to figure out the best way to arrange them for maximum space. Happy for a reprieve, she stretched out her aching muscles. Packing was harder work than she remembered, although really, this was the first time she'd ever had much worth packing. Increased pounding hurried her to the door. "I'm coming. Keep your pants on."

Impatient as always, Mollie had already let herself in by the time Jillian got there. Taking in the boxes, packing paper and all-around mess, she let out a long whistle. "You didn't waste any time getting started, did you?"

Jillian huffed at a curl that had escaped the bandanna she'd used to cover her hair. "No, I want to be ready to go as soon as I hear back on a job. And if you're here to talk me out of it, you can just leave now." Hands on her hips, she silently dared her friend to challenge her.

"No, I said I'd help, and I will. That doesn't mean I have to like it, or that I agree with what you're doing, but it's your life."

"Exactly."

Kneeling next to the box again, she gave up on efficiency and just piled the books in however they fit. It wasn't like boxes were hard to come by—the clinic got enough shipments of dog food and medications to keep her well supplied. "I'm doing the bookshelves first, then the pictures, then we can start on the hall closet."

True to her word, Mollie pitched right in, grabbing another box and a stack of books. "So, any leads yet?"

"A few nibbles. I have a phone interview with a place in New Mexico on Tuesday."

"New Mexico, huh? What about New York? Did you find any openings up there?"

"I didn't really look," Jillian lied. She'd spent quite a bit of time and ink printing job ads for New York City, only to toss them in the trash.

"Well, you should. If you're going to be selfish enough to move away from us, you should do it for a good reason. Moving to be with the man of your dreams qualifies. Running away, on the other hand, does not."

"I'm not running away, I'm getting a fresh start."

"You say to-*may*-to, I say to-*mah*-to."

"Juvenile."

Mollie stuck her tongue out, undeterred.

"And I'm not moving to New York City. First of all, Nic has given me zero indication that he has any interest in making things work between us."

"Maybe that's because he thought you would never agree to relocate. You made such a big stink about how Paradise Isle is the only place you've ever felt at home, he probably never even considered asking you to be near him. And yet here you are, moving away, leaving everything."

Mollie had a point. She had made it sound as though she would never leave, for anything. Until just a few days ago, she hadn't thought she ever would. But that didn't mean anything, did it? "It would be pointless, anyway. Even if I did move up there, which I won't, he's almost never home."

"Maybe he's never had anything worth going home for?"

"Right…gorgeous guy, lots of money, apartment in the city. He's been starved for female companionship, I'm sure." Her eyes rolled so hard she almost sprained something.

"Maybe not. But love is different, it changes things. If love is powerful enough to make you pick up and run from the one place you've always said you'd never leave, don't you think it would be enough to get him to spend more nights at home?"

All Mollie's talk of love was making her head spin. "He's not in love with me. Anyway, I'd probably hate a city that big. I've always said I want to start a family somewhere small, with a hometown feel to it. You know that."

"Sure, and that's a great dream. But it seems to me, you're looking at this from the wrong angle. What's important about a home is the people in it, not what zip code it's in." Shrugging her shoulders, Mollie went back to packing the box in front of her.

Jillian looked into her own box, then at the things still waiting to be packed. She'd spent so much time and energy searching out things that would make this apartment feel special, feel homey. But no matter how she decorated, it never had the kind of inviting vibe she was going for. Sure, she'd been burned by people in the past, but had that somehow taught her to invest her emotional energy into a place, instead of people? Was she so afraid of being hurt again that she'd ignored the importance of love in her search for the perfect home? So many times she'd prayed and hoped for a real family, but when had she stopped believing that wish would come true? Had she traded her dreams of love for security?

If that was her coping strategy, it wasn't working very well. Wasn't that why she tended to stay at work late, or go by Mrs. Rosenberg's in the evening? She thought about the houses she'd envied growing up—all were filled with people that cared about each other. Even the clinic, with all its sterility, felt welcoming because Cassie and Mollie were there. Despite herself, she had wonderful people in her life. Was she really going to let her old insecurities drive her into leaving them, running away from everyone that mattered, in a misguided attempt to protect herself?

Was that hidden fear the reason her romantic relationships had never gone anywhere? Because she was afraid of being abandoned again? Had she pushed Nic away, too, because of her distrust? Maybe she had been too quick to assume things between them could never work out, too quick to shut the door on what could have been. She had missed her chance to fix things with him, but that didn't mean she had to keep repeating the same pattern.

Energy rising, she stood, dumping the half-filled box, the books thudding to the floor. "You're right."

Mollie nodded, her short hair bouncing. "Always. But in what way, specifically?"

"About me, about people being more important than places. I've always said that I'd stay in Paradise forever, right? So leaving just because things are changing is crazy."

A smile filled her friend's face. "Totally insane. And stupid."

"Don't go overboard." She smiled. "But moving isn't

what I really want. Paradise might be different, but my friends are the same, and I'm not going to give them up." She felt her own grin growing. "I'm staying. Which means—"

"That we need to unpack all these boxes." Mollie sighed. "Do you have any wine? This is going to take a while."

Nic wasn't sure how long he had been in his father's office, alternating between pacing the floor and staring blankly out the window. Long enough that the offices had grown quiet other the bustle of the janitorial staff somewhere down the hall. He really should leave, but instead he sank into his father's worn desk chair. In front of him a small city of photographs populated the desk, as if guarding the stacks of paperwork enshrined there.

One, older than the rest, caught his eye. The frame was a plain, wooden square, aged but sturdy. The picture inside was faded, the sepia tones revealing two men, one middle-aged and bearded, the other young and clean-shaven with an adventurous gleam in his eye. Father and son shared similar dark features, features that Nic had inherited, as well.

He hadn't thought about his grandfather, his *nonno*, in quite some time. His health had kept him from visiting the past few years, but before that he had made a point of staying in touch with his descendants in America, despite the distance. Picking up the picture to look more closely, Nic could make out the bow of a boat in the background, one they had probably built together. Nonno had been a shipbuilder, as had his father before him. Lorenzo, Nic's father, had been taught the craft at a young age, with the expectation that he would continue the family tradition.

But the youngest Caruso had had other dreams. He'd worked for passage to America, sure his destiny was there. And it had been. He'd used his business expertise and natural charm to find jobs, saving until he could buy the rental home he'd been living in. He might have never owned more than a property or two, but wise investment and a healthy dose of luck had allowed him to channel his legendary determination into what was now one of the premier resort chains in the country.

And no one was more proud than Lorenzo's own father, who had made it his personal mission to stay in every single Caruso Resort. If he'd ever been upset about his son's choice to immigrate, Nic hadn't heard about it.

The family ties that spanned the two continents hadn't broken or strained over time, only strengthened. That was an accepted fact of Nic's family history, but one that he was now seeing through new eyes. There had been no disloyalty in his father's decision to leave the family shipbuilding tradition or the country of his birth. Maybe it had caused some tension; surely there had been concerns, but never hard feelings. So why did he feel so trapped by his own relationship with his father? Had he confused his connection to his father's business with his connection to the man himself?

Yes, his father had wanted a son to take over the business—he'd made no secret of that—but he'd also never indicated his love for his children hinged on it. No, the blame was his own. Success in business had become a way to prove his loyalty to his father, a way to earn his respect. And that was still important; it always would be. But following blindly in another man's footsteps, even a man as wise as his father, wasn't a life. It was time to make his own decisions. He needed to respect himself enough, trust himself enough, to follow his own heart.

His father had left part of his family on another shore, but in doing so he'd expanded the family in other ways. Vision finally clear, Nic grabbed the desk phone. Dialing from memory, he waited for her to pick up, fingers absently tracing the faded photograph.

"Hey, Isabella? We need to talk."

Chapter Sixteen

"Up you go." Jillian lifted the elderly schnauzer into a cage lined with clean, soft towels. Mr. Snappers was recovering from his dental extraction, and was still a bit loopy from the medication. She checked his IV again and adjusted the fluid rate, then placed a hot water bottle wrapped in a soft cloth next to him. The warmth would help him recover more quickly and would feel good to his old bones.

Finished with her midday patient checks, she washed her hands, then walked to the front desk to see if the first afternoon patient had arrived. Dan Jameson was there, talking to Mollie, his dalmatian focused on the cat cowering in a carrier a few feet away. "Hey, Dan, how's Flash doing?" The lanky, white-whiskered man was a security guard at the county courthouse, but volunteered with the small island's fire department and considered it his civic duty to keep the fire station mascot in good health.

"Right as rain, Miss Jillian, right as rain. I just stopped by to pick up his special food." Flash had a genetic condition that caused bladder stones; a prescription diet helped keep them at bay.

"Wonderful! And you're only giving him the special prescription treats now, right?"

"I keep a jar of them at the station house and some in my pocket for when we're out and about. The kids like to make him do tricks, and he likes to show off, don't you, boy?" He patted the handsome animal, pride showing in his face. They were a great pair, and an example of everything she loved about Paradise. How could she have even considered moving?

Mollie handed Dan his receipt and then turned to Jillian. "Dan was just filling me in on some news. It seems the sale of the Sandpiper is moving forward."

Her stomach tumbled as if tossed by a rogue wave. Counting to ten silently, she steeled her spine. If she was going to stay in Paradise—and she was—she would have to come to terms with the sale and the changes it unleashed. "Well, that was to be expected."

Dan shook his head. "Maybe so, but it sure seems to be happening fast. A lady over in the clerk's office told me that the survey was already ordered, and the seller is hoping to be done with it and back in Orlando within the month."

"I didn't think it could happen that quickly." She swallowed and reminded herself that the sooner it was done, the sooner Nic would be onto the next project and out of her life.

"Me, either, but I guess when you've got money, the wheels turn a bit more quickly than they do otherwise."

"I guess so." Rubbing Flash's silky ears, she sighed. Gesturing to the bag of food on the counter, she asked, "Can I take this out for you?"

Eyes wide, he shook his head. "No, ma'am, I can't have a lady carrying my things for me. The boys at the station would never let me live it down."

She laughed, recognizing the truth in his words. "I'll get the door for you, then, if it won't hurt your reputation too much."

"Just don't tell anyone." He winked, then hefted the bag without letting go of the waiting dog's leash. She beat him to the door, swinging it open for him, then took a minute to appreciate the breezy fall afternoon. A light wind stirred the palms that dotted the street and carried the smells of the Sandcastle Cakes with it. "Hey, Mollie, when's the next appointment due? Do I have time to run and grab a coffee?"

"You've got five minutes, but I just made a full pot, so why do you need to run out?"

She grinned ruefully. "Because I like my coffee with a side of pumpkin spice scone. I can smell them from here."

"Ooh, yum. Get me one, too. But hurry."

"I'm already gone. Tell Cassie I'll grab her one, too."

"Grab me one what?" Cassie asked, walking in past Jillian, returning from her lunch break.

"A scone and a coffee. The smell of pumpkin spice is too much to resist."

"Ooh, perfect. I knew I had a light lunch for a reason. Whose turn is it to buy?"

"Mine," Jillian answered. "I'll be right back."

Heading for the sweet shop across the street, she felt

her shoulders slide down, her tension over the discussion of the Sandpiper soothed by the normalcy of the errand. The new influx of tourists might make her daily coffee run take a little longer, but surely places like the Sandcastle would stick around, at least until one of the national donut chains chased the crowds and opened up shop. Grimacing, she entered the quaint storefront, where the warm aroma of sugar and spice reminded her of her mission.

"Something wrong?" Grace Keville asked, pausing from wiping down a gleaming display case chock full of decadent desserts.

"Nothing one of your delicious scones won't fix. Three pumpkin ones, please, and some cappuccinos to go with them." Sandcastle Cakes didn't offer the variety of coffee creations that The Grind did, but the freshness and sheer number of drool-worthy treats made it her favorite place for an afternoon pick-me-up. Her mouth watering, she scanned the glass cases. Scrumptious muffins, cookies the size of her hand, layer cakes dripping with buttercream. How did Grace stay so skinny? Just the scent of all that yumminess was probably adding an inch to each of her own thighs.

Seeing her order was ready, she tore herself away from the wonderland of confections. "Thanks, Grace, this is just what I needed."

"If only all my customers were so easily pleased." She wiped a smudge of flour from her face with the edge of her apron. "I've had to do three mock-up cakes for one of my wedding clients. If it's this hard to decide on a cake, I don't see how she ever managed to pick a groom."

Laughing, Jillian pocketed her change and took the cardboard drink carrier and white bakery bag. "Good luck with Ms. Indecision. I'd better go before Cassie sends out a search party for me."

Walking as quickly as she could without spilling coffee, she pondered how to protect small business owners like Grace from the influx of commercialism that was on the horizon. She'd bring that up at the next Preservation Society meeting; there might be zoning issues or other changes they could make if they hurried.

Unfortunately, it was too late to protect her heart; that was a restoration project with no end in sight.

Nic adjusted his tie for the umpteenth time, hoping his impatience wasn't overly obvious to the man on the other side of the desk. He'd dealt with dozens of mortgage officers at banks across the country, and they all seemed to move in the same lethargic time warp as this guy. The minute hand on the large wall clock ticked by with maddening precision, a metronome for the musical shuffling of papers and clacking of keyboards. No other deal had been this nerve-racking, but he'd also never had a deal with so much riding on it.

He needed this to go through smoothly, without any last-minute changes or red-tape snags. He'd spent hours going over the business plan, the revenue projections, the zoning regulations. Everything was there; he just needed this one poorly paid employee to stop overestimating his own importance and sign off on it. He'd seen the glint in the man's eye—he was enjoying making someone with the Caruso name wait on tenterhooks. It might be the only time he got to be in a position of power with someone like Nic, and he wasn't letting it go sooner than he had to. Recognizing the situation for what it was, Nic had forced himself to smile, to make small talk. And now, he forced himself to wait.

"Well…it seems everything is in order." The mousy man with thinning hair and an ill-fitting suit looked up. "I know you've called in some favors to fast-track this. I find that highly irregular, and not the proper way of things. But Mr. Ackerman, the bank president, has instructed me to proceed. Everything will be ready for you at the closing, as you arranged."

Thank heaven for small favors and the connections his father had made over the years. He needed this deal to close as soon as possible. He shook the man's limp hand and was out the door, on to his next appointment. He had a meeting with an architect in twenty minutes, and then a landscape specialist after that. If all went well, he'd have the big items on his list checked off by late afternoon and be back in New York by nightfall. He had some shopping to do, and the limited options on Paradise Isle just weren't going to cut it for this particular task.

He was almost to the architect's when he saw her. She had darted across the street, almost directly in front of where he was stopped for a red light. She hadn't recognized him in a different rental car, but he'd know her anywhere. Her dark curls bounced as she walked, and her cheeks were reddened by the wind. His body hardened as he watched her. Would it always be like this? Would he always want her, need her so badly, that just the sight of her nearly drove him mad?

A car honked behind him. The light had turned green without him noticing. He drove through the intersection, fighting the urge to turn around, to go to her. But that wasn't part of the plan. He had things he needed to do, and he couldn't let his hormones, or his heart, distract him.

He pulled into the small parking lot in front of Island

Architecture with five minutes to spare. Time enough to make a quick phone call.

"Hey, Dad, just finished up at the bank. Your phone call did the trick."

His father's voice rumbled back. "Are you sure you want to go through with this?" Concern echoed over the airwaves.

"I'm sure. The numbers make sense."

"It's not the numbers I'm worried about. You're more important to me than any of that."

"I know, Dad." And he did know. They'd had a long talk, late into the night, after he'd met with Isabella. They were on the same page now, and that felt good. Really good.

"I'll call you after the closing, let you know when everything's settled. And Dad?"

"Yes?"

"Thanks again for understanding."

"You got it. Now, get back to work. You've got a big project on your hands."

"You're right, I do. Bye." He hung up and did what his father had advised, what he did best. He got to work.

"I wish I had better news for you, but if there's a way around this, I can't find it."

Jillian absorbed the Preservation Society president's words, knowing they were no more than the truth. She and Edward had been poring over zoning regulations, municipal codes and city ordinances for hours, hoping to find something they could use to stop the spread of the large chain stores they both were felt was inevitable. It wasn't that she was averse to commercialism—she liked to shop as much as the next girl—she just wanted to protect the small businesses that gave Paradise so much character. She'd hoped there would be something already on the books, but it looked as though they'd have to start from scratch. A process that would take more time than they had.

She shouldn't have gotten her hopes up. She had been so sure they would find a way to protect the charm of Paradise amid the changes the new resort would bring. But the town's elected officials had never anticipated this kind of rapid progress; no one could have predicted this.

Heart heavy, her neck stiff from hunching over the conference table so long, she stood and stretched. "You're right, Ed. There's nothing more we can do about it tonight, anyway. I knew the Caruso lawyers would have triple-checked everything as far as the hotel itself, but I had wanted there to be something we could do about all the other changes coming." She started stacking up the books and reams of paper they'd torn through. "Looks like we don't have a leg to stand on."

"Don't give up just yet. I'll ask around, see if there's anything else we can do."

"Thanks, Ed. I'll try to stay positive.

"That's the way. Remember, the people here won't change, not just because there are a bunch of new stores and tourists crowding up the place."

"Good point, and exactly what I needed to hear." On impulse, she hugged him, making him blush like a schoolgirl instead of the middle-aged man he was. This learning-to-trust business was hard, but he was right. She needed to remember that the people wouldn't change just because everything else did. Maybe someday expecting the best from people would be second nature, but for now she appreciated the reminders. She'd probably need a lot of them as construction got under way. Leaving Ed flustered, but smiling, she said her good-byes and left the small library room that served as the society's headquarters.

At least she hadn't run into Nic yet. She was on pins and needles every time she left the house, certain she would bump into him on the street or in a café. The constant anxiety was draining her; she needed to relax. Maybe she'd check out a book before she went home, something lighthearted. Romance was out, but maybe one of those funny vampire books, where everyone wore designer clothes twenty-four hours a day. Something to take her out of her head for a bit.

Browsing the stacks, she found a few that looked in-teresting, and started for the checkout area. Reading the back cover of one of her picks, she walked right into one of the other patrons in line. "Excuse me, I wasn't look-ing where I was—"

"Jillian."

"Nic. Wow. I didn't expect to see you here. I mean, here, the library, not here, Paradise." Off-kilter, she tried to look anywhere but at his face. The book in his hand caught her attention. "*Native Florida Plants for the Landscape Beginner*, interesting choice. I hadn't pegged you as the gardening type."

"Just some research. How about you?" He gestured to the paperbacks she was clutching.

"Some pleasure reading." She tried to hide the covers from him. Why did all the novels have to feature such erotic images on the front? He was going to think she was sex-crazed if he saw them. Which admittedly was pretty accurate where he was concerned. They were in a library, of all places, and he still had her blood thrumming through her veins, her body warming in all the right places. At least the sudden jolt of lust offered a bit of a distraction from the ever-present ache in her heart. Hormones beat heartache any day.

"Good, you deserve a bit of relaxation."

"Seemed like a good idea. Things have been a bit stressful."

He winced at her not-too-subtle indictment. "I suppose I deserved that."

"Yes, you did." If only she could really hate him, that might make things easier. But she couldn't.

Moving forward in line, he handed his book to the librarian at the desk, presenting a Paradise Municipal Library card. When had he gotten that? The library did issue short-term cards to nonresidents for a fee, but not many people took advantage of the service. It seemed like a lot of trouble for a short-term business trip.

He wasn't planning on extending his stay, was he? He had to go. Soon. Being this close to him, and not having him, was agony. Even breathing hurt. He had to go so she could try to forget him and move on with her life. Every run-in would be like ripping off a newly formed scab. She needed space and time for the wounds to close, for her heart to mend.

He'd finished with his transaction, and was watching her, his eyes soft. "I had planned to call you tonight."

Keeping her face averted, sure he'd see the turmoil in her eyes, she handed her books to the impatiently waiting librarian. "I don't think that would be a good idea."

"No, I can see that." He hesitated. "Have a good night, Jillian."

Not able to trust her voice, she only nodded. Accepting her silence, he turned and walked out of her life once more.

Chapter Seventeen

Nic paced the whitewashed boards of the Sandpiper's wraparound porch. After that last run-in with Jillian, it was obvious that a straightforward approach wouldn't work. Hell, the way she'd treated him had him rethinking his plan altogether. Maybe he'd done enough damage and should cut his losses and run.

Except he wasn't built that way. For better or worse, he didn't quit, and he didn't walk away, not when it mattered. He might be making some changes in his life, but he was, at heart, still the same guy. Which meant he needed to find a way to get Jillian to listen to him, no matter how angry or hurt she was. She might push him away forever after that, but at least he would know he tried.

Frustration spurred him down the stairs and onto the soft sand of the beach below. Maybe a walk would clear his head. Leaving his shoes by the steps, he started for the shore. Then he went back and moved his shoes farther out of sight, under a step. He knew it was ridiculous—crime was almost nonexistent in Paradise—but New York habits died hard. It was going to take a while to adjust.

Satisfied he wouldn't be the victim of a random shoe-napping, he started off at a brisk pace. Most of the young families had already packed up for the day, and in their place were older couples walking hand in hand, enjoying a simple Friday night. He knew from the local paper that the beach was also a favorite of the high school crowd, come the weekend. He had read that one student had broken his arm on this beach, trying to play tackle football by moonlight. If that was the worst trouble the young people got into around here, he figured they were doing pretty well. This place really did seem like a tropical version of a 1950s sitcom.

His feet kept time with the waves, carrying him farther down the coast. Ahead, he spotted a dog chasing seagulls, barking in delight as they kept just out of reach. Smiling, he wondered what Murphy thought of the birds. He knew Jillian took him for regular runs on the beach; maybe they were old hat by now. He still couldn't get over how dedicated she was to that dog, caring for him better than many people did their own pets.

He stopped. Murphy—that was his answer. Jillian might not be willing to meet with him, but she'd do anything for Murphy. It was a dirty trick, but he just needed it to work once. Hopefully she'd agree the ends justified the means. And if not, well, he wouldn't be any worse off than he was now.

* * *

It turned out Mrs. Rosenberg loved his scheme and was happy to lend Murphy to the cause. When he'd spoken to her last night, she'd agreed to have the dog ready at five thirty today. She had already called Jillian to tell her not to stop by to exercise Murphy, saying she had family coming by that wanted to see him. All the other details were taken care of, and, checking his watch, he decided it was time to head over to collect the dog.

He had directions with him, but felt pretty confident he could find her house without them. He'd become much more familiar with the island over the past several days. Driving along the coast, he marveled yet again at the constantly changing view. Today he saw nothing but blue sky and a single osprey silhouetted darkly against it. The big bird was perched on a light post, where he, or she—he had no idea how to tell the sexes apart—had built an enormous nest. He'd seen quite a few of the precariously balanced constructions, and every time wondered how they kept the things from tumbling to the water below. Maybe he should pick up a book about the local birds the next time he hit the library. He'd never been much of a reader, but he'd been doing a lot of new things lately. Given the scope of his plans, it made sense to continue to research the area.

Turning onto one of the main thoroughfares, he kept an eye out for any businesses that might be interested in putting together vacation packages, things that could be bundled with a hotel stay. The dive shop seemed like a good bet, and maybe the kayak outfitter, as well. He was also hoping to work out some arrangements with local restaurants for picnic baskets to be delivered directly to the beach for lunching families. Driving by the photography studio's window display had the gears turning in his head, and he made a mental note to drop by with a business card and proposal next week.

Soon he was past the last of the commercial buildings and navigating the residential neighborhood where Mrs. Rosenberg's house was. The houses here were older than on the other side of the island. Most were small, single-story bungalow types with stucco or siding to protect them from the harsh Florida sun. Mrs. Rosenberg's was easy to spot, the pink paint standing out among the more neutral colors of her neighbors' homes. A few plastic flamingos were the only thing keeping her house from being a Florida cliché.

Shutting the car door, he started up the walk. At his knock, Murphy's enthusiastic barking greeted him, followed by Mrs. Rosenberg's muffled voice as she shushed the eager border collie. Once she opened the door for him, he held up a treat he'd stashed in a pocket. Murphy, knowing the routine, plopped his furry rear end on the floor, then accepted the treat with dignity. Nic ruffled the dog's fur and took the leash that Mrs. Rosenberg had already secured.

"Thanks again. I really appreciate you letting me borrow him."

Her brightly painted lips turned up as she regarded man and dog. "I'm happy to do it. I don't usually condone sneaky behavior, but it's for her own good. She has some issues with change, I know she does, but sometimes you have to embrace change if you want to move forward. Besides, if you don't take him, he's liable to drive me crazy, with her not coming to play with him tonight."

"Well, I'll take good care of him. Any particular time you want him back?"

"No rush. I went ahead and told the girls in my senior group to come over—didn't want to be lying to Jillian. We'll wait up together to hear how things go."

He had no doubt they'd be gossiping about it all night. Heck, there might even be bets placed. But at the end of the night, he would be the one taking the risks, and the stakes were high.

Jillian put the final coat of polish on her freshly manicured nails. The pretty golden color was unlikely to last, given how hard she was on her hands during the workweek, but it was a Saturday, and she figured she deserved a bit of pampering, even if she had to do it herself. The meticulous process also gave her something to focus on other than Nic Caruso, Caruso Hotels and the entire mess that had become her personal life.

Since she'd run into him, she had cleaned her apartment, decluttered her closet, baked and frozen more muffins than any one person could ever hope to consume, and gotten an early start on her Christmas list, thanks to the wonders of online shopping.

But no matter what activity she threw herself into, the pain was still there, gnawing away at her. There was an empty spot inside of her, a deep hole that no amount of manic cleaning or self-improvement could touch. Even when she closed her eyes, exhausted and desperate for sleep, she saw him. His dark eyes, chiseled jaw and teasing smile followed her into her dreams, dreams that left her needy and restless.

It seemed there was no cure for heartbreak, other than, hopefully, the tincture of time. She'd gotten through other disappointments, but this time was different. She had finally learned to open her heart, only to have it squashed like one of the many lovebugs stuck to her windshield.

Still, the hurting couldn't last forever. She'd just have to keep her chin up until then. She could do that. Focus on work, and her friends, and maybe take up a hobby or twelve. Reading hadn't worked; every hero in every story had reminded her of Nic. Maybe knitting or golf. Golf was popular.

She was searching golf lessons on the internet, and becoming increasingly intimidated by the prices, when the phone rang.

Desperate for a new distraction, she grabbed the phone without checking the caller ID. "Hello?"

"Hey, Jillian, it's Nic. Please don't hang up."

"Why not?" This was crazy—how many times did she have to tell him to leave her alone? Her stupid heart was beating a happy tune just hearing his voice, but her head knew there was only pain down that path.

"Because I need help, or rather Murphy does. He's here, running on the beach. I don't know if I can catch him on my own."

Well, crap. This was really starting to get old. She'd have to talk to Mrs. Rosenberg again about being more careful. "Fine. I'm on my way. Keep an eye on him until I arrive, and keep your phone on. I'll call when I'm there."

Fuming, she got her keys and stomped down the stairs. She was supposed to be pampering herself. Now, she'd be torturing herself instead, teasing her heart yet again with the one man she wanted but couldn't have. Maybe she needed to get away. Not move, she'd ruled that out as cowardice. But there was no reason she couldn't take a long-overdue vacation, maybe go camping in the state forest or drive up to St. Augustine for a few days. Anywhere would be better than here, if being here meant constantly running into Nic.

By the time she got to the Sandpiper, she had a vacation itinerary mapped out. She parked and noted that other than a few cars in the employee section, and a single rental car that must be Nic's, the place was empty. Odd, but then again, with the sale so soon, maybe they'd stopped taking reservations. Crunching over the gravel, she punched Nic's number into her phone. It rang three times before she got a breathless answer.

"Hey, are you here?"

"Yeah, walking up now. Are you still on the beach?"

"No. Yes. Just…come around to the back." And the phone clicked off.

He'd sounded a bit off; maybe Murphy was giving him trouble? Or maybe he wasn't thrilled to have to see her, given how she'd treated him the past few times. She'd blown hot and cold so often she felt like a hair dryer on the fritz. He had every right to be a bit wary of her mood. Or just frustrated to once again be saddled with a delinquent dog. Either way, she'd get Murphy, and herself, out of his hair as quickly as she could. Her pockets were stuffed with liver treats, more than enough to guarantee the canine's cooperation.

If only the human male could be wrangled so easily.

She took the steps two at a time, ready to get this over with so she could continue with the business of getting on with her life. The front door was right there, but it was just as easy to go around via the wraparound porch. Between cleaning, baking and pampering, she'd been cooped up inside for too long, and the longer route gave her a few more minutes to brace herself before she saw him.

Skirting potted orchids and patio furniture, she made the trek around the stately building. Not a single guest to be seen—in fact, if it wasn't for the murmur of voices drifting up from the beach, she would have sworn she was alone on the island.

Reaching the final turn, she saw Nic in one of the wicker lounge chairs, Murphy sitting expectantly at his feet. Surprised, she watched as Nic tossed the dog a treat, then ruffled his fur. Man and dog looked completely at ease, as if they were just enjoying the afternoon air. If there had been any kind of crisis here, it was long over. So why had he called?

Chapter Eighteen

Nic felt like a suspect waiting for a jury verdict. He'd prepared his case, would make his arguments, but in the end the decision was out of his hands. At least he had Murphy as a character witness.

Wait, was he really so far-gone that a dog was his best chance of success?

Sadly, yes, yes, he was. If an actual dog would keep him out of the proverbial doghouse, he wasn't going to fight it. He stroked Murphy's coat, more to calm his own nerves than settle the animal. In fact, Murphy seemed perfectly content. He figured the continuous consumption of liver treats probably had a lot to do with that, so he tossed the happy dog another one.

"You're going to make him sick if you give him too many of those."

Busted. "They're really small."

"And very rich. We'll take him home in your car. If he yaks, you can deal with it."

Nic looked down at the mostly empty bag of treats in his lap. Maybe he had been a bit overgenerous. Murphy nosed his leg, maybe to show support, more likely to search for more treats. "You heard her, no more."

"So, I thought you needed help. Seems like you're doing just fine on your own."

"I don't suppose you'd believe that I just now got him under control?"

"You're not sweating, he's not panting and it doesn't look like either of you have any sand on you at all."

Sand. He hadn't thought about that. Oh, well, the ruse had gotten her here, so it had served its purpose.

"Are you going to tell me why you dragged me over here?"

Her blue eyes were like icicles, her lips pursed in righteous indignation. She was angry as hell, and still knock-you-on-your-butt gorgeous. Her mood didn't matter when it came to his feelings, or his libido. He wanted her, in his arms, in his life, in his bed. But wanting didn't mean having. If he didn't play his cards right, she was going to walk out of his life, leaving him right back where he started. And he wouldn't, couldn't, let that happen.

"I had to show you—and tell you—some things. If you give me this, I promise I won't bother you again. I'll leave town tomorrow if that's what you want."

She narrowed her eyes. "If I listen to you now, you'll leave town? No more running into each other, no more emergency phone calls, no more anything?"

"You have my word. You tell me to leave, and I'll go."

Sweat trickled down his back. Everything was on the line—there would be no second chances.

"Fine. Let's get this over with."

Not exactly a vote of confidence, but he'd take it. "Come with me, we'll walk Murphy while we talk."

"While *you* talk. I don't have anything left to say."

"Either way." He started to reach for her hand, but figured that would be pushing it. Instead, he grabbed Murphy's leash and headed around the side of the building, hoping she would follow. She did, and his lungs loosened a bit. Drawing a deep breath, he spoke. "As you can see, the structure of the building is sound, but a lot of the siding needs to be replaced, and in several places the porch railing shows signs of dry rot." He gestured to an area where the weathered boards, bleached by the sun, were peeling away. "The good news is I've found a contractor who has experience working on buildings from this time period. He should be able to match everything, make it look just like the original."

Jillian stopped dead. "Replace? What's the point of replacing stuff when you're just going to tear it—"

"No questions yet. I'm not done, and you promised to listen."

Jillian's mouth opened, then closed. He definitely had her interest now.

"There are obviously some improvements that can be made inside as well—a new computer system, some upgrades in the kitchen, that kind of thing. More updating than remodeling. But really, what I wanted to talk to you about are the grounds." He chanced touching her, taking her elbow to steer her down the stairs to the walking path below.

"The majority of the land is undeveloped. Other than

a few fruit trees, and of course the benches and paths, nothing had been touched out here."

"Right. Your point?" She was still prickly, but he could tell she wanted to hear more.

"Well, I'm thinking we can add some interest to the landscape and still keep the natural feel of the place. For instance, a butterfly garden with a gazebo at the center. There's a nursery on the mainland that can set one up using native plants. It will add some color, but blend in with the natural surroundings."

"A gazebo?"

"Yes, I think it's exactly what we need, if we want to hold weddings here again. Didn't you say this used to be a popular place for them?"

"Yes, but wait—what about the giant resort?" He could almost see the wheels turning in her head. Grinning, he ignored her question and continued walking, taking her past the parking lot to the south side of the inn.

"Take a look at this spot." He pointed to a shady clearing amongst the scrub pines. "What do you think of a playground here, the kind made mostly of wood, so it doesn't stand out too much? Maybe some picnic tables or benches for the parents."

"Playgrounds. Gazebos. Weddings. New siding. Am I crazy or are you? Because I don't see how any of this makes sense when you're just going to bulldoze the place."

"Maybe I'm crazy, maybe I'm not. But I one thing I can say for sure, no one is bulldozing this place."

"Excuse me?" Jillian felt as though she were on some kind of carnival ride, her head was spinning so fast.

Nothing made sense. She had to have heard him wrong or misunderstood. "I could have sworn you just said you aren't going to tear down the Sandpiper."

He gave her a smug little grin and tucked his thumbs in his pockets, as if there was nothing strange about her question or the whole situation. "That's right. I'm not tearing it down. It's got good bones and a history. I don't want to lose that."

"But, then, what are you going to do?" She suddenly understood how Alice felt when she fell into Wonderland. Up was down, down was up and the man in front of her was mad as a hatter.

"That's what I've been trying to talk to you about. For starters, we'll remodel the inn itself, repair what we can and replace what we can't. That's the easy part."

"None of this sounds easy."

"Easy in that we already have a blueprint and the contractor just has to replicate what's already here. No big changes. It's the rest of it that I wanted your input on."

"My input?"

"That's right. I want to bring the Sandpiper back to its glory days, and to do that I need to know more about it. I need to know what the community is missing, what it needs and wants. You know Paradise better than anyone, so I thought you would have some insight into what needs to be done."

She had some thoughts all right, but getting them sorted out would take a while. "Let me get this straight. You are not going to tear down the Sandpiper or build some giant luxury hotel?"

"Right."

She plowed on, trying to grasp what was happening. "And you called me—tricked me, in fact—to come out here, so that I could tell you where and how to build a playground?"

"Among other things, yes."

He really was insane. It was the only explanation.

And now he was walking away, veering off the path and cutting through the clearing he'd designated for the playground. She scrambled after him, catching up to him in a grassy area that backed up to the bluffs, with a view of the beach below. Grabbing his arm, she spun him toward her. "You said other things. What other things?" How much more bizarre could this get?

"You said there used to be community events here. What kinds?"

"Well, charity stuff, mostly. They used to sponsor a yearly fish fry benefit for the library and a chili cook-off for the fire department." She tried to think of what other events she had attended over the years, as well as the ones she'd heard about from Cassie from before she'd moved here. "There used to be a big Christmas tree lighting every year, with caroling and hot chocolate. And I think there was a fall festival, too, but that was before my time." She looked out over the ocean, spotting a cruise ship against the horizon. "They would do the fireworks here, too, on the Fourth of July. Sometimes there was a pig roast or a clambake first."

She turned back to him, and realized he was actually taking notes on a small notepad. "Did you get all that? Or should I repeat it for you?" She tried to infuse as much sarcasm as possible into her voice, but he either didn't pick up on it or tuned it out.

"I got the basics. But thanks." He tucked the pad into the back pocket of his slacks. "Next question. What do you think about this spot for a house?"

"Whose house?"

"The innkeeper's house, of course. There's a suite in the Sandpiper, but I'm thinking that a house makes more sense. It opens more room up for guests in the main inn and offers some privacy for starting a family."

"I can't imagine Caruso Hotels makes a habit of building custom homes for the management staff."

"No, but Caruso Hotels doesn't own the Sandpiper. I do. And I want a house."

Her knees buckled, and she leaned against a well-positioned pine. The rough bark scraped through her thin T-shirt, grounding her. He bought the Sandpiper? Not Caruso Hotels? He was staying? Permanently? There would be no way to avoid him, not if he was running the inn. And what was that he said about starting a family? Was she going to have to watch him date, get married, have children? She'd said she would stay in town, but how could she do that when Paradise was turning into her own personal version of hell?

Jillian looked as though she'd been sucker-punched. The color that had heated her cheeks while they argued had vanished, leaving her as pale as the white clouds floating overhead. Eyes wide, she stared at him. Maybe he shouldn't have blindsided her, but she hadn't left him much choice. She never would have come if she'd known that he, not his father's company, was the new owner of the Sandpiper. Still, her silence had his gut churning. "Are you okay?"

She nodded, straightening almost imperceptibly against the tree she was braced against. "You don't mean you bought it for yourself, right? You must mean you bought it on behalf of Caruso Hotels."

"No. I couldn't do that if I wanted to, since I'm no longer an employee of Caruso Hotels. I turned in my resignation the last time I was in New York."

"But...you can't just quit. You're a vice president, for crying out loud. "

"Not anymore. My sister Isabella now has that title, and good luck to her."

"Your sister? I thought she worked at some fancy Wall Street investment firm."

"She did, but she hated it. She was tired of doing work in the background, never getting to make a decision. She wanted something different, and with her business background and her degree, she'll do a great job."

Jillian threw her hands up, more flustered than he'd ever seen her. "But, it's not just about the job—it's about who you are."

"Who I was. I don't want to be that person anymore." He shoved a hand through his hair. How could he explain this to her, when he was just starting to figure it out himself? "I wasn't living my own life. I was just doing what I thought everyone wanted me to do, what I thought I had to do. But that's not a real life, and it's not what I want. I need to do something for myself, find my own path."

"And that means being an innkeeper?"

"It's as good a job as any. I can use what I know about the industry, but be truly involved. I won't just be setting things in motion. I'll get to follow through. I can create my own vision, instead of following someone else's. And I'll get to put down real roots. I'm tired of living out of a suitcase."

The shock and horror on her face were easy to read, but hard to accept. He had planned on her being surprised, but the anguish on her face, that was something else entirely. Had he misunderstood everything? Imagined her feelings in order to justify his own? He'd convinced himself that she was fighting the same losing battle he was, but maybe she was already over him or had never really wanted him in the first place.

No. He couldn't think like that. Couldn't go there. He'd second-guessed everyone he loved too many times, trying to live up to expectations they'd never really had. If he'd learned anything in the past few days, it was that the only real freedom came from honesty. He had to act on what was in his own heart and then let the chips fall where they may. At least he would have no regrets.

"What about your family?"

"My family wants me to be happy. I don't know how I convinced myself that the only way to make them proud was to be a part of the family business, but I know now that isn't true. I did some hard thinking about our family and what has kept us all together. It isn't the business or a set of expectations. It's love."

He took a deep breath to steady his nerves. His eyes searched hers; he needed her to see the truth in his words.

"I stayed in the job because of love. And I left it for love, because love is the most important thing in the world. I bought the Sandpiper for love, for you. Because I love you."

He saw the tears coming, and before he could stop and think, he took her in his arms. She clung to him, her shoulders shuddering as she sobbed. At a loss, he stroked her hair and let her cry herself out, wanting nothing more than to keep her protected in his arms forever.

* * *

Jillian couldn't believe she was blubbering all over Nic, but she was powerless to stop. All the worry and pain and sadness had built up, and now, hearing his words, she couldn't hold it back anymore. It flowed out of her on a river of tears, clearing the path for the warmth that was taking over, everywhere her body touched his. Was it possible? Pushing away, she wiped her blurry eyes. She had to hear it again, had to know he'd really said it, that it wasn't her emotions playing tricks on her. "You did all this because of me? Because you love me?"

"I did it for us. I bought it for us. I wanted to show you how I feel, and the Sandpiper seemed like the perfect way to do that. You love it, and I love you. Pretty simple."

"But...you really love me?"

He laughed. "Were you not paying attention?"

"I just need to hear it again." Her voice was shaking, one more thing out of her control. "I've never heard it before."

He smiled. "That's because I've never said it to you before. But I'll say it again. I love you."

Something fluttered inside, breaking free. She felt the tears starting again, but this time she laughed through them. "No, I meant I've never heard that before, from anyone." She smiled. Were her feet even touching the ground? "I'm glad you were the first."

Taking her trembling hands, he pulled her against him. "I'm so sorry, I didn't think... With foster care, your parents. I just didn't think. I should have said it before now, but I promise I'm going to make it up to you. I'm going to say it so often you'll get sick of hearing it."

Stopping, he tilted his head to the side. "Wait, does this mean you love me, too?"

She stretched onto her toes, angling for a quick kiss. Lips nearly touching, she whispered against his lips, "I love you—"

He took her mouth, silencing her. She responded eagerly, no longer afraid of the feelings he triggered. When his tongue teased, she parted for him, letting him explore her mouth, answering him with her own bold invasion, needing to taste and feel and love the way she had wanted to since she first saw him standing at the door of the clinic. She held nothing back; she gave him everything. Heart and soul went into that kiss, and he met her passion moment by moment, until her head was spinning and the only thing keeping her upright were his arms firmly wrapped around her body.

Slowly, gradually, he gentled the kiss, nibbling at her bottom lip before putting a few inches of distance between them. "I have more I want to show you, tell you."

"More?" She felt half-drunk; how much more could there be? She had everything she wanted right here, in him.

"Plenty more, of everything," he answered, his husky voice sending shivers through her body. Practically giddy, she let her imagination paint pictures of what could be.

"But for now, let's start with where we should put the gazebo. I want you to pick the spot."

"Me?"

"Didn't I say I bought this because of you? You're the one that knows it, that loves it. You should be the one that helps it come alive again. Besides, a gazebo is all about romance, and as the female of the species I'm willing to bet you have more expertise in that particular area."

"Hmm, I suppose that's true." She grabbed his hand, dragging him with her as she looked for the perfect spot. "You said it would be used for weddings, right?"

"Right."

"Okay, so you want a good view and enough room around it for guests to gather." She nearly floated across the grass, heading for what she knew would be the ideal location. Tucked away, just off the walking path, was an open area framed by towering palms and a clear view of the ocean. "Here," she declared confidently.

"You're sure?" He squeezed her hand.

"Positive. It's the perfect setting. The sea as a backdrop, plenty of room for folding chairs, easy access from the parking lot—this is the spot."

"Well, if you're sure." He walked to the center of the spot she had chosen, Murphy following at his side. Pulling a small box out of his pocket, he knelt down on one knee and looked up at her.

"Wait…what are you doing?" He couldn't be… could he? Even Murphy looked confused, his gaze going from her to Nic and back again before finally laying his head on Nic's bent knee, as if waiting to find out what was happening.

"I told you, I want to start holding weddings here again. And I want the first wedding to be ours, if you'll have me." He held out a ring, the large diamond scattering rainbows as it caught the setting sun. "Jillian Everett, will you marry me?"

Her throat closed over another round of tears, stealing her voice. Pulling air into her lungs, she swallowed and tried again. "Yes." And then, offering a shaking hand, "When?"

He laughed, the hearty laugh she'd learned to love, and slid the ring over her trembling finger. "As soon as we can get the gazebo built, if that's what you want."

Tugging on their joined hands, she pulled him back up, leaning into his body. "Nic?" She slowly kissed her way along his jaw, letting her hands roam his back, his chest, his arms.

He groaned; whether in frustration or pleasure, she wasn't sure. "What?"

"Build fast."

Chapter Nineteen

Nic figured he'd probably broken a world record in gazebo construction, if there was such a thing. He had ended up having to order most of the supplies—there wasn't much of a lumber selection in Paradise—but once everything had arrived he had attacked the project like a man possessed.

He had spent years supervising construction, massive projects with hundreds of crew members. But this was the first time he had actually built something from the ground up on his own. When the last board was in place and the last coat of paint applied, he was as proud of it as he ever had been of a high-rise hotel.

Of course, it turned out that planning a wedding involved more than just building the gazebo. Thankfully, Jillian was handling most of the other preparations. He was much more at home wielding a hammer, however inexpertly, than he was in a florist's shop. He'd be forever grateful that his main contribution was preparing the physical surroundings.

With the gazebo finished, he had turned his energies to the Sandpiper itself. The previous owners had canceled all the reservations, and the hotel was isolated enough that there was no one to disturb as he hammered and sanded and painted until the wee hours. They were going to hold off on the grand reopening until after the wedding, but he wanted the old building to be at its best when his family came for the ceremony. His parents, siblings, aunts, uncles and maternal grandparents would be on hand, filling the Sandpiper to capacity. His father's parents weren't able to make the transatlantic trip on such short notice, but they had insisted the happy couple visit while on their honeymoon tour of Italy. He had been so afraid of losing his family, but the upcoming wedding had only brought the generations closer together.

Checking his watch, he decided he had enough time to shower before the last of them arrived. He'd just finished moving his things into the suite he and Jillian would be living in while their new house was built. Construction was slated to start next week, but for now this little grouping of rooms would be home. Their home. The irony of living in an inn after protesting his suitcase lifestyle for so long wasn't lost on him. But now, instead of moving on, he'd be putting down roots, becoming part of the community.

More important, he'd have Jillian at his side—and in his bed. She'd suggested, since they had already waited so long and the wedding was so soon, that they should wait to make love until after they had said their vows. Something about heightening the anticipation. He, as a gentleman, had agreed, but after three weeks of sleepless nights and countless cold showers he was regretting that particular act of chivalry. As far as he was concerned, anticipation was highly overrated.

At least they wouldn't have far to go. They had decided to spend their wedding night here at the Sandpiper before catching a plane for Rome tomorrow afternoon. The less time between the saying of the vows and the consummation of the marriage, the better. If he had his way, they'd skip the reception entirely and go straight to that part, but that wasn't going to fly with Jillian or their guests.

Forcing himself to think of something other than getting his soon-to-be wife in bed, he stripped down in the large bathroom they would soon be sharing. Waiting for the water to heat up, he eyed the shower stall. They could probably both fit in there, with some creative positioning. Steam rose as he contemplated the possibilities.

But this was no time for fantasizing; he had a wedding to get to. Resigned, he braced himself, and turned the faucet to cold one last time.

"All set?" Cassie asked, straightening Jillian's veil.

Jillian nodded. She'd been ready since the moment Nic had asked the question. But as excited as she was to marry him, she hadn't wanted to give up her girlhood idea of a dream wedding, either. So, with Cassie and Mollie's help, she had crammed months of wedding preparations into a few short weeks. Now, after what felt like a mad dash to nuptial bliss, she was more than ready to get to the "I do" and become the newest member of the Caruso family.

She had worried that Nic's parents would resent her,

blame her for him leaving the company. Instead, she had been inundated with offers to help with the wedding. Both of his sisters and his mother, Marie, had flown down as soon as they heard of the engagement to take her dress shopping. Then, while everyone else was oohing and aahing over her final choice, Marie had quietly made arrangements with the shop owner to pay for it herself. She'd insisted that it was her honor, making Jillian cry for what was probably the hundredth time since Nic had proposed.

Now they were all waiting for her, seated around the beautiful gazebo Nic had crafted. She just had to walk down the path and her new life would start.

Taking a deep breath, she watched Cassie and then Mollie, dressed in simple pastel gowns, walk down the aisle to the strains of a single violin. Then Emma, in the pink flower girl dress she'd picked out herself, started down. She held a posy of flowers in one chubby hand and Murphy's leash in the other. The canine ring bearer trotted beside the pretty girl, trained to home in on Nic, his new master. Mrs. Rosenberg had given them the dog as their first wedding present. There was a mountain of gift-wrapped boxes waiting for them inside, but nothing else could compete with him.

When the music shifted to the traditional wedding march, Doc Marshall, Cassie's father, gave Jillian's hand a squeeze. "We're on, sweetie. Your fella's waiting."

Taking his arm, she let him guide her out of the trees and into the clearing. Nic, in an elegant linen suit, waited for her in the gazebo he'd worked so hard to build. As she started down the aisle he smiled, the love in his eyes unmistakable.

The officiant said the standard words, and she was

sure there were readings and hymns and all the usual things. But all she heard were the vows they said to each other, and the declaration that they were man and wife. And then even that proclamation was wiped from her mind when Nic's mouth met hers in their first kiss as husband and wife.

The rest of the evening was a blur of tears and laughter, new family and old friends. Finally, as the stars came out, the guests began to make their farewells.

"Miss Jillian, you forgot!"

Jillian looked down from her plate of cake at a very sleepy Emma. "What is it, honey? What did I forget?"

"The flowers. You forgot the flowers."

Jillian looked around at the garlands artfully decorating the wraparound porch. "There are plenty of flowers, Emma, enough for you to take some home even, if you want."

The little girl furrowed her eyebrows. "No, not these flowers. The ones you throw. So someone else can get married."

"Oh, the bouquet. You're exactly right, princess. I did forget the bouquet. Were you hoping to catch it?

Wide-eyed, she shook her head, curls swinging. "No, I don't wanna get married. I wanna help you throw it."

Laughing, she tucked the child's hand in hers. "Okay, let's do it."

She found Cassie quickly and told her the plan. Then, upstairs, she led Emma out onto the main balcony, handing her the bouquet of tropical blossoms. "Here you go, Emma. I'll pick you up, and on the count of three, you throw it as hard as you can, okay?

The little girl's eyes beamed. "Okay."

Shouldering the girl, she saw Cassie and Emma, Nic's

sisters, and even Mrs. Rosenberg gathered on the lawn with the other single ladies. As soon as the crowd spotted the duo on the balcony they started the countdown. "One—two—three!"

The cheer that went up almost drowned out Emma's shout of "Mama, catch!" But everyone saw her smile when the bundle of flowers landed directly in Cassie's hands.

"Now it's all over, right, Jillian?" the tired girl asked, stifling a yawn.

All but the best part, Jillian thought, suddenly as eager as Emma to move the guests along.

It took another hour, but finally they were standing on the front steps, waving goodbye to the last of their guests. Even the cleaning crew had finished, leaving only Nic's family, most of whom had already retired to their rooms.

"Good night, Jillian, and welcome to the family." Lorenzo Caruso, the last to go up, gave her a crushing hug, squeezing a laugh from her.

"Thank you so much. And do let us know if you need anything during the night."

"Are you kidding? It's your wedding night. My wife and son would kill me if I even thought about disturbing you."

"You've got that straight," Nic agreed, wrapping his arms around her. "Now go, before Mom comes looking for you."

"Nic!"

"No, he's right. He's waited long enough to have his bride to himself. We'll see you in the morning." He patted her arm, then retreated into the inn.

The minute the door was shut, Nic swung her around,

pressing her against the railing, his mouth coming down hard on hers. A throbbing hunger rose up at his touch, and tasting him only made it stronger. His hands crushed her dress as he molded her to him. Maybe she should care that he was ruining the lace, but she was too desperate for his touch to stop him.

Her own hands sought skin, pulling and pushing at the layers of formalwear. "Nic, I need—" she panted in his ear.

"I know, baby." His husky voice vibrated along her neck, sending chills zinging along her skin. In an instant, she was in his arms, being carried across the threshold and up the stairs, into the master suite.

They somehow managed to undress as they tumbled onto the bed, buttons flying, mouths nipping, hands seeking. He expertly teased her to a fast peak, leaving her gasping and aching for him. "Now, Nic, please, now."

And then they were one, and it was everything she had ever wanted or needed. He whispered words of love as she met his pace, then urged him on. Perfectly matched, they raced for completion together, each swallowing the other's cries as they climaxed.

Afterward, he rolled her on top of him, so her head rested on his chest. Hearing his heart galloping, she smiled and snuggled closer.

"Don't get too comfortable, Mrs. Caruso. That was just the opening act," he rumbled, stroking lazy patterns up and down her bare skin.

"So was the wait worth it?" she teased.

"Let just say we have a lot of work to do, to make up for lost time." As if to punctuate his words, she felt him growing ready again.

"Speaking of time, I know it probably makes more sense to wait to start a family until the house is built—"

Cutting her off with a kiss, he flipped her beneath him. "I can build fast, remember? Nine months should be plenty of time."

* * * * *

T19

MILLS & BOON®
The Italians Collection!

2 BOOKS FREE!

Irresistibly Hot Italians

You'll soon be dreaming of Italy with this scorching six book collection. Each book is filled with three seductive stories full of sexy Italian men! Plus, if you order the collection today, you'll receive two books free!

This offer is just too good to miss!

Order your complete collection today at
www.millsandboon.co.uk/italians

MILLS & BOON®

Why shop at millsandboon.co.uk?

Each year, thousands of romance readers find their perfect read at millsandboon.co.uk. That's because we're passionate about bringing you the very best romantic fiction. Here are some of the advantages of shopping at www.millsandboon.co.uk:

Get new books first—you'll be able to buy your favourite books one month before they hit the shops

Get exclusive discounts—you'll also be able to buy our specially created monthly collections, with up to 50% off the RRP

Find your favourite authors—latest news, interviews and new releases for all your favourite authors and series on our website, plus ideas for what to try next

Join in—once you've bought your favourite books, don't forget to register with us to rate, review and join in the discussions

Visit **www.millsandboon.co.uk**
for all this and more today!

MILLS & BOON®

Cherish™

EXPERIENCE THE ULTIMATE RUSH OF FALLING IN LOVE

A sneak peek at next month's titles...

In stores from 16th October 2015:

- **Housekeeper Under the Mistletoe** – Cara Colter *and* **Coming Home for Christmas** – Marie Ferrarella
- **His Lost-and-Found Bride** – Scarlet Wilson *and* **The Maverick's Holiday Masquerade** – Caro Carson

In stores from 6th November 2015:

- **His Texas Christmas Bride** – Nancy Robards Thompson *and* **Gift-Wrapped in Her Wedding Dress** – Kandy Shepherd
- **The Prince's Christmas Vow** – Jennifer Faye *and* **A Husband for the Holidays** – Ami Weaver

---